"A joy to read."
—*RT Book Reviews* on *Christmas Cowboy Duet*

"Ferrarella's romance will charm with all the benefits and pitfalls of a sweet small-town setting."
—*RT Book Reviews* on *Lassoed by Fortune*

"Heartwarming. That's the way I have described every book by Marie Ferrarella that I have read. *In the Family Way* engenders in me the same warm, fuzzy feeling that I have come to expect from her books."
—*The Romance Reader*

"Ms. Ferrarella warms our hearts with her charming characters and delicious interplay."
—*RT Book Reviews* on *A Husband Waiting to Happen*

"Ms. Ferrarella creates fiery, strong-willed characters, an intense conflict and an absorbing premise no reader could possibly resist."
—*RT Book Reviews* on *A Match for Morgan*

* * *

We hope you enjoy this dramatic new miniseries:

The Coltons of Texas: Finding love and buried family secrets in the Lone Star state...

If you're on Twitter, tell us what you think of Harlequin Romantic Suspense! #harlequinromsuspense

Dear Reader,

Welcome to a brand-new saga of the Colton family. This story has everything. A bride murdered on her wedding day, a patriarch (Matthew Colton) who, as an imprisoned serial killer, will never be in the running for Father of the Year. You have the man's family, seven siblings who were torn from one another and scattered to the four corners of the foster care system when their father murdered their mother. These same siblings struggled against all odds to rise above the sins of their father to come into their own and win back the respect of the community, all while trying to find out just where this man hid the body of their late mother so they can finally put her to rest. Matthew Colton will tell them—but only if they agree to play his little game. Each month, the terminally ill killer will dispense one clue to a different sibling, which, once put together, will lead them to their mother's body. Added to this is the fact that there seems to be a new serial killer on the loose, emulating Matthew's old MO, and the Coltons are afraid that it might just be their youngest sister, whom no one has seen for the past six years.

As I said, this story has everything—except for you. So come, read, second-guess the motives behind everything that's happening, and enjoy!

As always, I thank you for taking the time to read one of my books. Without you, there would be no stories. And, from the bottom of my heart, I wish you someone to love who loves you back.

Love,

Marie

COLTON COPYCAT KILLER

Marie Ferrarella

HARLEQUIN® ROMANTIC SUSPENSE

Special thanks and acknowledgment to Marie Ferrarella for her contribution to The Coltons of Texas miniseries.

Recycling programs for this product may not exist in your area.

ISBN-13: 978-0-373-27970-8

Colton Copycat Killer

This edition published by arrangement with Harlequin Books S.A.

For questions and comments about the quality of this book, please contact us at CustomerService@Harlequin.com.

Printed in U.S.A.

This *USA TODAY* bestselling and RITA® Award-winning author has written 250 books for Harlequin, some under the name Marie Nicole. Her romances are beloved by fans worldwide. Visit her website, marieferrarella.com.

Books by Marie Ferrarella

Harlequin Romantic Suspense

The Coltons of Texas

Colton Copycat Killer

The Adair Affairs

Carrying His Secret

Cavanaugh Justice

The Cavanaugh Code
In Bed with the Badge
Cavanaugh Judgment
Cavanaugh Reunion
A Cavanaugh Christmas
Cavanaugh's Bodyguard
Cavanaugh Rules
Cavanaugh's Surrender
Cavanaugh on Duty
Mission: Cavanaugh Baby
Cavanaugh Hero
Cavanaugh Undercover
Cavanaugh Strong
Cavanaugh Fortune

Visit the Author Profile page at Harlequin.com for more titles.

To
Melissa Senate,
with love,
for handing me
a great outline
to work with!

Prologue

"Watch and learn, little sister. Watch and learn."

Celia Robison's eyes met her younger sister, Zoe's, in the full-length mirror as the former fussed over her wedding veil, adjusting it for the umpteenth time in order to best play up her delicate features.

She was talking to Zoe in the church's bridal room. The latter had popped in a few minutes ago to see how she was coming along. Celia always loved having her sister around—and never more than today—because she knew she always looked even hotter and sexier than usual in comparison. The sweetly attractive Zoe looked like the typical shrinking violet that she was.

Right now, Celia was approximately ten minutes away from leaving her single status permanently behind and marrying Sam Colton, a rather stoic detective on the Granite Gulch police force—and a man that Zoe had secretly been in love with since forever.

Not even Sam knew how she felt, and the librarian—a rather stereotypical career choice that suited the shy, blond-haired Zoe rather well—intended to keep it that way. She doubted Celia knew how she felt about Sam when her sister had asked her to be one of her bridesmaids—and Zoe knew she couldn't turn her sister down without arousing suspicion. Besides, with both of their parents gone now, Celia was the only family that she had. So, much as it made her heart ache, she'd said yes.

The charade—pretending to be happy for Sam and Celia—was really killing her despite the brave front she was putting up. But this mysterious, cat-ate-the-canary look on Celia's face had caused her to forget her own bruised heart and piqued her curiosity.

To be honest, it made her uneasy.

Celia had always been the devious one, but given her looks, she had always been able to get away with things others in her position wouldn't have been able to.

"Watch and learn what?" Zoe finally asked when Celia said nothing further. Her sister just continued smirking at her reflection, as if some huge secret existed between her and the mirrored image.

"Why, how to trap a man of your choice, of course, little sister."

Zoe hated that condescending tone. Celia used it often with her. "What are you talking about, Celia?" Zoe asked impatiently.

Celia turned away from the mirror to look at her. "Why, Sam, of course. I'm talking about Sam. My future beloved." She laughed then, clearly delighted with herself.

Zoe moved in closer, discreetly sniffing the air between them. "Have you been drinking, Celia?"

"Not yet, but I will be soon," Celia assured her with a wink. "That's what got him, you know. Drinking. And now I'm going to be wrapping him around my little finger—him and that lovely Colton money of his."

Zoe was beginning to get a very uneasy feeling in the pit of her stomach. Something was very off. "English, Celia, speak English."

Celia blew out a breath, and shook her head. "You know, you really *are* no fun, Zoe. Lucky for you I'm in such a good mood."

As if to underscore what she'd just said, Celia began softly humming the bridal march under her breath.

This one time, Zoe didn't allow her sister to put her off. She intended to get to the bottom of this. Celia seemed too pleased with herself for it to be some inconsequential trivial thing.

"What did you do, Celia?" she asked in a firm, quiet voice, her eyes never leaving Celia's.

Of the two of them, Celia was the vivacious one, the one who had always turned heads. The one who could have any boyfriend she wanted and who could talk her way out of anything. Celia was just that stunning.

As for her, Zoe knew she had to content herself to live in Celia's shadow. But for the most part, she was okay with that. She loved her sister, even though at times that wasn't nearly as easy as it should have been.

But what Celia was alluding to was sending an icy cold shiver down her spine and Zoe intended to find out just what her sister was talking about.

Now.

"You seem very pleased with yourself, Celia." Flattery had always been the way to go with her sister. "Why don't you tell me why?"

Celia looked as if she was just bursting with her accomplishment and utterly enthralled with what she'd managed to do. "Sam's marrying me to give his baby a name."

Zoe's eyes opened so wide, they almost hurt. "What baby?"

"Exactly," Celia countered smugly, her eyes dancing.

Zoe caught hold of her sister's shoulder to keep her from turning back to the mirror. "Celia, stop speaking in riddles. You're going to be marching down the aisle in a few minutes. Tell me what you're talking about."

Had she thought it would do any good, she would have issued an ultimatum to her sister—that she couldn't leave the small room until she came clean. But Zoe knew Celia would only laugh at her and then it would get ugly from there. All she could hope for at this point was to wear Celia down.

"You do take the fun out of things, you know that, right?" Celia accused, annoyed. And then she laughed. She was far too pleased with herself to let the occasion be ruined by her annoying younger sister—who did, after all, have her uses. "Sam and I never even slept together."

Zoe's mouth dropped open. "I don't understand. If you didn't sleep together, then why would he think you're carrying his baby?" Something was really, really wrong here.

Celia sighed. Spelling it out took a little of the drama, not to mention fun, out of it.

"Because one night, after he'd killed that awful criminal he'd been chasing, he came to my place just to unwind and talk. Seems killing doesn't sit well with Sam," she added with offhanded sarcasm. "Anyway, he was upset and I just kept plying him with whiskey until he totally passed out on my sofa. Then I messed up my place to make it look like we made wild, passionate love all over the living room. When he woke up, I *shyly* told him I'd never done 'anything like that before.'"

That in itself was a lie, Zoe thought. Celia had slept with several men who she knew of in the past couple of years. There'd probably been more.

"Two months later, I came to his place and tearfully told him that I was pregnant with his baby." Her grin all but split her face. "That's when he offered to 'do the right thing,' just like I knew he would," Celia said, absolutely pleased with herself. And then she spread her arms wide and declared, "And here we are."

Stunned, Zoe didn't even know where to begin to unravel all this. "Then you're not—"

"Nope," Celia responded. Zoe didn't think it was humanly possible to be more pleased with herself than Celia was at this minute.

Didn't Celia realize the dangerous game she was playing? *We both know Sam wouldn't put up with being lied to*, Zoe thought.

She asked the first logical question that occurred to her. "What happens when the full nine months go by and there's no baby?"

Celia waved away the very idea she was suggesting. "Oh, I'm not going to wait the full nine months. Sometime in the next month or so, I'll tearfully tell him I lost our baby. Who knows?" She laughed with a careless half shrug. "He might even be relieved. And by then, it wouldn't matter anyway—I'll be married," she concluded.

Since Zoe had dropped her hand from her shoulder, she turned away from her sister and went back to adjusting her veil and dress.

"I really do make a beautiful bride," Celia complimented her reflection with feeling.

"You can't get married to Sam under that pretext," Zoe cried, staring at her in disbelief. "You have to tell him the truth."

"No, I don't." And then Celia looked at her in the mirror, her face almost contorted with anger. "Oh, stop carrying on like this. After all, it's not like Sam believes in love or marriage or even the almighty institution of family." She paused to put another layer of lipstick on. "So marrying a woman he doesn't love isn't such a big deal."

"And you're okay with that?" Zoe asked incredulously. This had to be the lowest thing her sister had ever done, tricking someone into marrying her. "Marrying someone who isn't in love with you? You're *really* okay with that?"

Celia's temper was just about at its end. "*Of course* I'm okay with that. Do you know how rich those Coltons are?"

"I don't care if they're richer then God," Zoe exclaimed. "You can't go through with this, Celia. It's not right," she insisted.

Celia tossed her head in that way of hers, the way that emulated queens ruling over small kingdoms.

"It's more than 'right,' it's perfect," she countered, completely pleased with what she had brought about. "Now stop lecturing me like some dried-up old spinster with a house full of cats and get ready for the biggest bash this town has seen, bar none."

Zoe pressed a hand against her stomach, which was suddenly twisting itself into a tight knot. She felt sick to the bottom of her stomach. She couldn't be a party to something like this.

Celia, Zoe noted, had gone back into her own little world. Having eyes only for the image she beheld in the mirror and once again humming a tuneless

"Here Comes the Bride," Celia didn't even seem to hear her slip out of the room.

Her stomach twisted harder, threatening to make her throw up. She had to find Sam, find him and tell him what Celia had just confessed to her. Sam couldn't be allowed to go through with the ceremony. He'd be marrying Celia under false pretenses.

He'd be—

She came to an abrupt halt mentally. The thought of telling him about this elaborate scheme of her sister's made her feel even sicker. Moreover, if she went through with it, it would easily brand her as a snitch. She was the blameless one here, but that wouldn't be the way Sam would see it.

She had to try one last time to get Celia to call off the ceremony and tell Sam why on her own.

Squaring her shoulders, Zoe closed her eyes for a moment, trying to gather her courage together. She'd always just gone along with everything before, but this was the proverbial straw. It was just too much. She couldn't allow this wedding to take place.

Though she dreaded butting heads with Celia, that was exactly what she was going to have to do.

Eyes opened again, Zoe marched back down the hallway to the bridal room. Knocking once, she didn't wait for an invitation to enter.

Instead, she threw open the door, took one step into the room—

And started screaming.

Chapter 1

Zoe didn't remember screaming.

Didn't remember pursing her lips or emitting the loud, piercing sound less than a heartbeat after she'd opened the door.

Didn't remember crossing over the threshold into the room, or bending over Celia, who was lying faceup on the floor.

The exquisite wedding dress her sister had taken such all-consuming delight in finding was now ruined. There were two glaring gunshot holes in her chest and her blood had soaked into the delicate white appliqué, all but drenching it. The pattern beneath it was completely obliterated.

The whole scene, which was whizzing by and moving in painfully slow motion at the same time, seemed totally surreal to Zoe, like some sort of an ill-conceived, macabre scene being played out from an old-fashioned B-grade horror movie about a rampaging slasher.

And if the dreadfulness of all this wasn't enough, someone—the killer?—had gone on to draw a bizarre red bull's-eye on Celia's forehead. There was a single dot inside the circle, just off center, and whoever had drawn it had used some sort of a laundry marker, so the bull's-eye stood out even more than it normally might have.

This can't be real, it just can't be real.

The desperate thought throbbed over and over again in Zoe's head. She'd just left Celia, what, a couple of minutes ago? Five minutes, tops?

How could all this have happened in such a short period of time?

Who could have done this to her sister?

Why hadn't she heard the gunshots when they were fired?

And for God's sake, what was that awful noise she was hearing now?

Zoe tried to see where it was coming from, but for some reason, she just couldn't seem to turn her head.

She couldn't even move.

The noise was surrounding her. It sounded like wailing, or, more specifically, like keening. It approximated the sound that was heard when someone's heart was breaking.

Zoe had no idea the noise she was attempting to place was coming from her.

* * *

"You realize this is probably going to be the happiest day of your life, you lucky son of a gun." The declaration, uttered by one of the men waiting to be ushered down an aisle and into a pew, was directed at the bridegroom. "It's all downhill from here," the older man chuckled.

Detective Sam Colton kept the half smile he had been sporting for the past half hour pasted on his handsome, tanned face and merely nodded.

Words were not his strong suit and he couldn't think of anything to say in response to that, other than the fact that if this was to be the happiest day of his life, it certainly didn't put the bar up very high.

And as for it being "downhill from here," well, he already knew that.

He was marrying Celia Robison, who some of the other detectives on the force had made very clear they regarded as being quite an eyeful, as well as a number of other clichéd descriptions.

None of that had entered into the reason why he was standing here, waiting for everyone to take their seats so the ceremony could begin. Waiting for all this to be over with.

He was marrying the woman for one reason and one reason only.

She was having his kid and he'd vowed a long time ago that if he ever did happen to have any kids—most likely by accident, which this was—he was sure as hell going to be there for him or her. He wanted this kid's upbringing to be completely unlike his own. His childhood had involved his father killing his mother and then his siblings and him being scattered to the winds.

More specifically, they had all been sent off to different foster homes, but they might as well have been scattered to the winds for all the time they'd managed to spend together during all those awful, soul-scarring years.

No matter what it took, *his* kid wasn't going to go through that, wasn't going to feel abandoned, alone and ashamed because no one wanted him or her. If he had to marry Celia for that to happen, well, so be it. He'd managed to survive all this time—and had gotten as far as he had—by learning to roll with the punches. He'd roll with this one, too.

And in the end—

Sam's head jerked up as everything within him went on high alert the second he heard it.

Part of his response was due to his police training, the rest had evolved based on pure survival instincts. The latter had been necessary in order to live through some of the foster home stays he'd been forced to endure.

"Did you hear something?" Ethan, one of his brothers—they had pretty much managed to find one another and reunite in these past few years—asked him.

By now, Sam had broken into a run and ran past him without responding.

"I'll take that as a yes," Ethan said, answering his own question and hurrying after Sam.

Once they reached the hall, it was obvious the sound was coming from the bridal room. It grew louder and more jarring the closer they got.

"It's bad luck to see the bride before the wedding," Ethan called after Sam. It wasn't meant to stop his brother. Ethan was just stating a point of fact.

The next moment, as he came to a skidding halt behind Sam and took in the scene Sam was viewing, he muttered under his breath, "And this has got to qualify as the worst possible kind of luck a groom ever encountered."

For an excruciating, shattering moment, Sam froze several steps away from Zoe. At first, he wasn't even aware she was the one screaming.

He couldn't take his eyes off Celia.

It wasn't a sense of loss that was echoing through every fiber of his being. It was shock. Complete, total and utter shock, swaddled in disbelief. The shock was not tied to the fact that Celia was dead, but to the symbol he was looking at on her forehead.

He knew that symbol.

He recognized it from both photographs he'd seen originating from crime scenes, and from the nightmares that had haunted his earlier dreams.

That was the symbol his father, the infamous serial killer, Matthew Colton, used to draw on the foreheads of his victims.

But those victims were all men of a certain size

and age who reminded Matthew of his older, far more successful brother, Big J. It had been Matthew's way of doing away, by proxy, with a man whom he hated with every fiber of his being and whom he blamed for everything that had gone wrong in his life.

Matthew killed men, not women. The thought echoed over and over in Sam's head. And while Matthew had killed his wife when she stumbled across his heinous secret, he hadn't made a practice of killing young women in their twenties. If nothing else, it would have come to light by now if he had.

Besides, Matthew Colton had been behind bars for twenty years. He couldn't have killed Celia.

Then who had?

This didn't make any sense.

The detective in Sam wanted to focus exclusively on the murder—Celia was clearly already dead—of the woman whom he would have married in ten minutes. The human side of him that was struggling to resurface after being buried for more than twenty years felt obligated to offer some sort of comfort to Celia's sister.

Zoe looked as if she was bordering on going into shock—if she wasn't already there.

"Zoe—" Sam began, then fell silent, at a loss as to what to say next.

But he didn't have to talk. The moment he said her name, she turned toward him. He saw the tears flowing from her eyes and the stricken look on her face just before she collapsed into his arms.

He barely caught her in time.

Sam held on to her awkwardly, as if he felt that making any sort of contact would wind up cracking his carefully built up, impenetrable walls.

"She's dead," Zoe sobbed. "I was just in here and now Celia's dead. Why did I leave her? She'd still be alive if I hadn't left the room. Oh, God, why didn't I stay?" she sobbed.

Sam looked over her head helplessly toward Ethan. He knew what to do at a crime scene, knew how to defend himself against a killer and knew how to handle himself in all the steps between. But when it came to dealing with something like someone else's grief, or a woman's tears, he hadn't a clue.

Completely at a loss, he looked toward his older brother for help.

Ethan picked up his cue effortlessly. "Why don't you come outside, Zoe, get some air?" he suggested gently, trying to take hold of Zoe's arm. He was ready to lead her out of the room.

But Zoe surprised even herself and remained firm. She shook her head adamantly from side to side.

"No, I can't leave, I can't leave Celia," she insisted, looking down at her sister's prone body.

Sam had already felt for the pulse he knew was no longer there. Celia was gone. Whoever had fired the shots knew exactly where to aim.

Rising to his feet, Sam took a firm hold of Zoe's arm. "You can't do her any good anymore, Zoe. Celia's dead."

"But why? Who?" Zoe cried, looking at Sam through fresh tears.

Her last thoughts of Celia had been angry ones. Her last words had been condemning ones.

How was she supposed to live with that now?

The guilt of that—and of leaving Celia alone to fall prey to her killer in the first place—had already begun to eat away at her.

"Those are my questions exactly," Sam replied evenly. There wasn't a shred of emotion evident in his tone as he asked her pointedly, "What can you tell me?"

"Sam, don't you think now isn't the time—" Ethan began, trying to get Sam to treat Zoe with a little more compassion. Ethan's question indicated he thought the victim's sister looked as if she was a hair's breadth away from coming unglued. Asking her questions right now might just push the poor woman over the line.

But Sam apparently didn't see it that way.

"Now is *exactly* the time," Sam emphasized, looking at Ethan. "While it's all still fresh in her mind." And then he turned back to Zoe. "Zoe?" he asked, looking at her pointedly. "Did you see anyone walk into Celia's room after you left her?"

Zoe shook her head, wisps of blond hair coming undone and falling about her face and neck. "No," she responded hesitantly. "I don't think so..."

"You don't *think* so?" Sam demanded, stretching

out the key word and making it all sound almost like an accusation.

It only caused Zoe to look even more bewildered and at a loss.

"I don't know. I can't remember," she cried. "Everything's just a huge blur."

And the fact that it was, frustrated her beyond words. She would have raked through her brain with her fingernails if that would have somehow helped bring the missing details back into focus.

With Ethan looking on, Sam tried another approach. "All right, why did you walk out in the first place?" he asked.

She looked at him, stricken. How could she tell him what he wanted to know, knowing it would only humiliate him, embarrass him? Hurt him?

She would rather die herself than do that to him, especially at a time like this.

Dead or not, Zoe concluded, Celia didn't deserve a man like Sam.

"Zoe, why did you walk out?" Sam repeated more forcefully when she didn't answer him.

"We had an argument," she finally answered in a low, quiet voice.

"About what?" he pressed.

"Nothing important," Zoe told him, waving the subject away as fresh tears threatened to choke her for a second time.

Ethan attempted to step in again. "Sam, her only sister's just been murdered. She's clearly in shock.

She should see a doctor, not be interrogated right now. And yes, I know I have nothing professional to fall back on like Ridge or Annabel, or Chris—or even Trevor," he said, mentioning their other siblings, all of whom, unlike him, were in some branch of law enforcement. "But maybe you shouldn't be the one investigating this murder to begin with."

Sam gave him a look that most of the law enforcement agents in Granite Gulch had learned to steer clear of. "My town, my case."

"Your fiancée," Ethan countered.

Sam completely ignored the last detail. Instead, he looked at Ethan pointedly. "Did you happen to notice the mark on her forehead?"

Ethan had focused on the gunshots that had ended Celia's life and then on the victim's screaming sister. Now that his attention had been directed to Celia's forehead, Ethan looked and was immediately stunned.

Like a man in a trance, he raised his eyes back up to Sam's face. "Oh my God, is that—?"

"Definitely. Just like his signature mark, except the red dot's off center." Sam paused, staring at the bull's-eye. "That might mean something."

"Yeah, that the old man hasn't figured out how to be in two places at once," Ethan said, pointing out the obvious. "He's in prison, Sam, where he's been for twenty years."

"*Almost* twenty years," Sam corrected. He was a stickler when it came to facts.

Ethan conceded the point. "Either way, he couldn't

have done this. Besides, the old man only killed men who reminded him of his brother. Celia would have never been mistaken for a man, even in the dark." The second the words were out of his mouth, Ethan suddenly realized that Zoe was still in the room. "Oh, God, I'm sorry, Zoe. I didn't mean—"

But Zoe waved his words away. She was far too numbed by what had happened to take offense at something so trivial.

"It's all right. I understand. And I want to help." She looked from one man to the other. "I want to help any way I can to find who did this to Celia."

"Right now, you can help by going and getting yourself checked out by a doctor," Sam told her, undoing the bowtie he had put on under protest for the wedding. He took his cell phone out of his pocket and began to put in a call for backup.

"I don't need to be checked out," Zoe maintained stubbornly. "I didn't hit my head. I found my sister, murdered. I don't think the doctor's got any kind of medication to treat that." She took a breath, struggling to center herself. "I'm sorry about screaming like that before."

Sam shrugged. "Under the circumstances, it's understandable."

"Okay," she said, moving on. "What can I do to help?"

It was obvious that although she'd always been regarded as the meek sister and as far as he knew, she had always kept pretty much out of the way and in the shadows, Zoe was not about to just fade away until such time as he could get around to questioning her at length.

But he definitely didn't want her underfoot, either.

"Okay, you want something to do?" he asked her.

She was almost eager as she said, "Yes."

"Tell everyone out there that due to circumstances beyond everyone's control, the wedding's been called off—but they can't leave, because someone has to take down their statements." He spared her a preoccupied look. "Do you think you can do that for me?"

For as long as she could remember, she'd always hated having to break bad news to anyone, let alone an entire gathering of people who had come expecting to have a good time. But this was something that clearly needed to be done and Sam was asking her to do it. She put her own discomfort aside and nodded.

"Yes, sure, of course. And I'll tell them how very sorry you are that this happened and they had to be put through this."

Slowly checking out the victim, aka his bride-to-be, for a second time, albeit more thoroughly, Sam was already preoccupied. Zoe's words were only half registering as he looked up at her.

Belatedly, he realized what she'd just said. "Oh, yeah, why not?" he said.

"That's Sam's way of saying 'yes,'" Ethan prompted helpfully, giving her an encouraging smile.

Zoe flashed a very small, weak smile at him in response. "Yes, I know."

Ethan looked after her for a moment as Zoe left the room. "I think they used to call that kind of thing 'plucky,'" he commented to Sam.

"Yeah, whatever," Sam muttered, his mind far more preoccupied with the body before him and the murder it so clearly represented.

In all honesty, he hadn't wanted to marry Celia and had felt almost resentful she had somehow managed to trap him in this arrangement. But he certainly hadn't wanted to see her dead.

A sliver of guilt accompanied his thoughts before he pushed it—and those thoughts—away.

Sam rose again, knowing that more definitive information would be forthcoming from the medical examiner's autopsy. He was already impatient to get his hands on it and the ME and his crew hadn't even arrived yet.

"Definitely the same," he said under his breath, more to himself than Ethan. "And yet, different."

Ethan felt he should be there for him, seeing as how Sam had just lost his bride-to-be, but there were times he found it hard to get close to Sam. His younger brother had constructed an entire wall around himself and so far there were no cracks and no passkey.

We all fight our demons in different ways, Ethan thought. And those demons, he knew from experience, all bore their father's face.

"Well, that makes it as clear as mud," Ethan told his brother.

Sam laughed shortly, even though there was no

humor in the situation. "I know," he said. "That's what I'm afraid of."

There was sympathy in Ethan's eyes as he touched his shoulder. When Sam turned toward him, a silent question in his eyes, Ethan said, "In case I don't get a chance to say it later, I'm sorry."

His mind going in a dozen directions at once, Sam asked, "About what?"

Confused by his brother's response, Ethan gestured toward the body on the floor. "About your fiancée," he said pointedly.

"Oh."

For a second, he'd forgotten. This was a homicide and he was thinking like a homicide detective. Personal thoughts weren't allowed to enter into that. He'd trained himself that way.

"Yeah. Thanks." Sam shot out the words one at a time in staccato fashion, leaving his brother to wonder exactly what had gone on between Sam and the woman he could no longer marry.

Was Sam *that* good at hiding his grief, or had what had happened to all of them so long ago destroyed Sam's ability to feel anything at all, not even sorrow, much less love?

Ethan was almost afraid to find out the answer.

Chapter 2

When she opened the door leading into the church where the actual wedding ceremony was *supposed to be* taking place, someone automatically cued the organist. Strains of "Here Comes the Bride" began to swell throughout the church and everyone sitting in the pews automatically rose to their feet and faced the back of the church.

Half a beat later, as Zoe continued to stand there, all but frozen in place, someone from within the crowd declared in disappointment, "Hey, that's not the bride, that's Zoe."

The observation was immediately followed by a myriad of questions, all fired at once at Zoe who, since she wasn't the missing bride, was expected to satisfactorily field the various inquiries.

"Where's Celia?"

"What's going on?"

"How long does it take for that woman to get ready? Let's get this show on the road already."

There were more questions and more irritated complaints, but those were entirely indistinguishable to Zoe. Shouted out, they mingled with one another until everything just became one huge, pulsating cacophony of noise.

Standing there, with one of the double doors closed at her back in order to afford her support—her knees still felt incredibly weak and she worried about them buckling—Zoe cleared her throat and tried, at first in vain, to get everyone's attention.

Because her voice was initially so whisper soft, no one even heard her make the attempt except for a couple of the wedding guests who were closest to her at the rear of the church.

But others saw her lips moving and assumed she was telling them something.

"What?"

"Speak up!"

"I can't hear you!"

"What the hell is going on here?" someone from the center of the crowd roared angrily, their voice louder than the rest.

It was the last disembodied question that caused Zoe to stiffen in response. Angry now, as well as incredibly upset and shaken, she raised her voice as she made a second attempt to be heard.

"There's not going to be a wedding," she began.

Her voice was still somewhat shaky, but at least it was finally becoming audible.

"I drove all that way for nothin'?" an indignant woman cried angrily in response.

"What do you mean, there's not going to be a wedding?" someone else demanded heatedly.

"Why the hell not?" yet another, deep male voice wanted to know.

As close to losing her self-control as she had ever come, Zoe raised her voice again and shouted, "Because there's been a murder!"

Her voice cracked on the last syllable the moment she uttered it.

A sense of horror dropped over the gathering like an old-fashioned, heavy theater curtain made of asbestos.

"A murder?" someone near the front of the church cried. "What do you mean, a murder? Like with a dead person?"

A man two pews over spoke up. "No, she's kidding. Right? This is what they call black humor or something, right? She's doing this because Celia's not ready."

"Is that what you're doing? Stalling until the bride's ready?" a third person, a woman near the rear of the church challenged. "'Cause I don't know about anybody else, but I'm getting real hungry just sitting here, waitin'."

As the questions and retorts continued to fly fast and furious at her, Zoe gave serious thought to a full-on retreat. The wedding guests who had previously risen to greet the bride were still on their feet and more than a few were coming toward her, as if shortening the distance between them and her could somehow make what she was saying clearer to them—or better yet, transparent.

Zoe fumbled for the doorknob behind her, thinking to hold on to it and possibly swing the door open again in case she had to execute a very hasty retreat and create a temporary barrier between herself and the wedding guests who were quickly growing more annoyed by the second.

With her hand behind her back, Zoe wasn't able to secure the doorknob, but she suddenly felt the door opening behind her. She knew she hadn't managed to do that.

Was there someone behind her?

The next moment, her suspicions were confirmed as she heard Sam's deep voice addressing the agitated wedding guests.

"No one's stalling," he informed them in a voice that was not to be argued with. "There's been a murder and you all need to take your seats again." It wasn't a request, it was an order. "Someone from the police department is going to be coming to each and every one of you to take down all of your statements," Sam briskly told the wedding guests in his no nonsense voice.

"*All* our statements?" one of the guests questioned in disbelief.

Both rows of pews were filled to capacity, which in turn translated to a great many statements that needed to be taken. It could literally take hours before anyone was allowed to leave.

"All of them," Sam replied in a cool, concise tone of voice.

Someone closer to the rear of the church was definitely not satisfied with so little information. "Sam, what's going on here? We came here to see you get married. Who was murdered?"

Zoe made a judgment call. Sam didn't look as if he was willing to answer that question just yet, but she didn't think it was right to withhold the information. These people were supposedly Celia's friends. Still struggling to come to terms with what had happened practically under her nose, Zoe took the initiative and answered for Sam.

"Someone shot Celia."

Out of the corner of her eye, she saw Sam fire her a look that would have definitely kept her silent had she seen it first.

Her immediate reaction to it was to offer Sam an apology for having overstepped her bounds.

But any words to that effect never made it past her lips as anger uncharacteristically took over, vanquishing her tendency to just meekly accept whatever was happening rather than protesting it.

The first volley in that particular battle had been fired when she'd held her ground against her sister, wanting Celia to confess to Sam that she had engineered the lie about being pregnant just to trick him into marrying her.

Having spoken up then, she couldn't just quietly hold her peace now, especially when doing so—just because it was expected of her—made absolutely no sense to her. It was just cruel.

After all, this wasn't the kind of secret that someone was going to take to their grave. On the contrary, everyone was going to know who was murdered in a matter of hours, most likely in a manner of minutes.

What was the point of holding back?

It made no sense to her. Right now, she desperately needed to find something that made sense so she could hang on to it and rebuild her world which was, at this moment, completely decimated into charred, gray ashes.

Another disjointed chorus of voices was shouting out stunned reactions to the bombshell that Zoe had just dropped.

"Celia?"

"Oh my God, Celia's been shot?"

"Celia's really dead?"

"This is a joke—right?"

"Who did it?"

Sam had remained standing next to Zoe. He raised his hands now and gestured for the guests to lower their voices and in essence, cease asking questions altogether. Any further questions were all going to be coming from him, starting now.

From him and from the rest of the officers he had just called in to act as his backup.

"That's what we're going to be trying to find out," Sam informed the sea of faces that were turned toward him. "Now, this'll go a lot faster if you all just get back into your seats and wait until someone comes by to take down your statements."

"But we were all in here," one of the older women protested helplessly. "We didn't *see* anything."

"And if that's the case, it'll go even faster," Sam replied. His tone of voice, neither friendly nor accusatory, gave nothing away.

The church was now filled with several more patrol officers from Granite Gulch in addition to the detectives and officers who had been invited to the actual wedding ceremony. The latter group also included Sam's older sister, Annabel, who was a police officer on the same force.

The incoming officers joined forces with the law enforcement agents who were already there to make the process of questioning the temporarily captive wedding guests as painless as possible.

Growing just the slightest bit calmer, Zoe looked at Sam after he had finished briefing the newly arrived police officers.

"Who do you want me to give my statement to?" she asked.

Mindful of what Ethan had said to him earlier about the shock she was dealing with, he looked at Zoe with what he felt might very well be remotely associated with concern. After all, Zoe *had* been through a lot, and Celia was—or had been, he corrected himself—her sister. Moreover, though he didn't have any proof at the moment, his gut told him that Zoe had nothing to do with Celia's tragically dramatic end.

"Are you sure you're up to this now?" he asked Zoe, scrutinizing her closely. He was a fairly good judge of what a person on the fringe looked like. He'd sent enough of them there during interrogations.

Zoe curled her fingers into her hands and dug her nails into her palms, as if registering that pain could somehow help her maintain control over the grief running rampant all through her.

"Yes," she answered in a small, but firm voice. "I am—but thank you for asking."

He hardly took note of the last part. Glancing around the church, he took in the scene.

A handful of law enforcement agents from the small precinct had scattered throughout the pews, singling out wedding guests the way cowboys cut out cattle from a herd for branding. Every available police officer and detective currently there was clearly busy and would remain so for the next foreseeable several hours, if not more.

That essentially made up Sam's mind for him, although, in all honesty, it had pretty much been made up the moment he had found Zoe in the same room as Celia's body.

"You can give your statement to me," he told Zoe crisply.

Glancing around again, he looked for somewhere a little more isolated where he could interview the victim's sister in private.

When he spotted the reverend, he issued Zoe a quick order, "Come with me." He made his way over to where the preacher was standing near the front of the church, comforting several of his regulars, people who always attended Sunday services without fail. The parishioners were clearly distraught.

"Reverend Rimmer," Sam began as he approached the older man.

He got no further. The tall, thin man of the cloth immediately made his excuses to the trio he was talking to, cut the distance between himself and the groom and took hold of Sam's hand in both of his. For a thin man, he had very large, capable hands.

The moment the reverend began talking, it was obvious he had misunderstood why Sam had sought him out.

"Sam, I am so sorry this terrible thing happened. If you need to talk—"

"I do, but not to you right now, Reverend," Sam said, cutting the man off before the reverend could get wound up. "Would it be all right to use your office?" He nodded at the woman on his right. "I need to take Ms. Robison's statement and I need someplace where we won't be interrupted."

"Yes, of course, of course." But rather than step

out of the way as Sam had expected him to, Reverend Rimmer turned toward Zoe and took hold of both of Zoe's hands in his.

"Zoe, please accept my heartfelt condolences on your tragic loss. I didn't know your sister as well I would have liked—I didn't see her at Sunday services very often," he explained, "but I know she was a good woman who had love in her heart for her family and friends."

Zoe offered the man a smile, patiently taking in his words. She knew what the reverend was saying to her had to be his "go-to" comfort speech, offered to the family and friends of deceased people whom he had never gotten to know on a personal basis.

To the best of her knowledge, the only time her sister ever turned up at any Sunday services in Rimmer's church was when she was guaranteed a number of cute, eligible young men were in attendance, as well. During those rare occasions, Celia always arrived just a little bit late so she could make an entrance as well as an impression.

Celia always loved being the center of attention, Zoe thought. She felt it was her due.

In a way, Zoe thought now, if it hadn't ultimately involved her death, Celia would have reveled in the attention this whole thing going on now was generating for her.

But Zoe knew Reverend Rimmer was doing the best he could under the circumstances, trying to comfort her on the death of her sister. This all had, after all, happened under his roof, so to speak, and she felt bad for the preacher.

"If you need anything, anything at all," Reverend Rimmer was saying to her, "please don't hesitate to give me a call. Mrs. Rimmer and I are entirely at your disposal—day or night," he added, and for what it was worth, Zoe believed him.

"Thank you, Reverend," Zoe replied. "I'll be sure to keep that in mind."

Gently disengaging her hands from the preacher, she turned to a somewhat surprised-looking Sam. Taking a breath, she said, "Let's get this over with."

He'd known Zoe for a lot of years. Just how many, he couldn't have honestly said. But in all that time, he had only been vaguely aware of her. Still, she had never struck him as someone who spoke up, who could hold their own, especially not against a crowd. When he'd sent her off to inform the guests that the wedding had been called off, he'd just thought of her as a messenger. He hadn't thought anyone would give her a hard time.

He certainly hadn't thought she could actually *stand up* to anyone.

Live and learn, he thought now.

He spared her a quick glance. "This way," he instructed, taking Zoe by the elbow and guiding her out of the crowded area.

He'd gotten the church's layout just the other day, when Celia had dragged him to meet with the reverend to make the final arrangements for the splashy wedding she had made abundantly clear she had always wanted.

As far as he was concerned, they could have exchanged two-minute vows in front of some justice of the peace. He had absolutely no desire to have witnesses to something he wouldn't have done on his own in the first place. But since he'd made up his mind to do right by her and especially to do right by his unborn child, they were to exchange vows in front of people who were all one and the same to him at this point.

He didn't care. He'd just wanted it over with.

And now it is, he thought in an almost accusatory tone.

He forced himself to focus on the moment and not the past.

"The reverend's office is this way, down the hall," he told Zoe.

Releasing her arm, he led the way down the narrow passageway.

Compared to the rest of the church and its connected areas, the hallway was almost tomblike in its silence. The lighting that came through the windows located eight feet off the ground was strained and diffuse. Nothing about it was welcoming in Zoe's opinion.

"Kind of eerie," Zoe noted, stifling an unbidden shiver that shimmied up and down her spine.

"You don't have to be afraid," Sam responded almost automatically, then assured her, "Nobody's going to hurt you."

Although he wasn't carrying his primary weapon,

because he was supposed to be off duty and the tuxedo afforded no place to carry the heavy piece, he still had his backup weapon strapped to his ankle. Wearing it beneath the tuxedo trousers had been a challenge, but in the end, he had managed.

He thought of the old adage, "Where there's a will, there's a way."

"I'm not afraid," Zoe replied, waving away the suggestion that she was. "But it is eerie here," she pointed out. That feeling was only heightened by the crime that had just taken place there.

Arriving at the reverend's office, Sam tested the doorknob. The door wasn't locked. Even so, he looked carefully around and then entered the tiny alcove of a room first.

Caution trumped chivalry every time in his book.

A quick visual sweep of the area assured him there was no one in the small, rather claustrophobic room. Shelves crammed full of books of all sizes and shapes lined three of the four walls, adding to the intensely cramped feeling.

The reverend's desk was no different from the rest of the room. It had piles of papers and folders stacked around, behind and in front of an antiquated computer someone had donated to the church. The piles of paper and the computer succeeded in taking up all the available space on the desktop.

There were papers on the chairs, as well. At first glance, they looked to be preventing anyone from making proper use of the chairs.

Sam cleared off what was obviously the reverend's chair and then turned his attention to the only other available one in the office. He put both piles of paper on the corner of the desk as carefully as possible, sincerely hoping there wouldn't be an avalanche.

Finished, he gestured toward the chair and then suggested, "Why don't you take a seat." When Zoe did so and he had followed suit, he said to her, "In your own words, why don't you tell me exactly what happened before you left your sister—and then what you saw when you came back."

The knot in her stomach returned, tightening and threatening to cut off her very air supply.

She didn't want to tell him what Celia's last words to her had been.

Chapter 3

Zoe folded her hands in her lap and for a moment, she just focused her entire being on breathing.

Once she had taken in and exhaled several deep, cleansing breaths, she raised her eyes to Sam's and addressed his request—at least in part.

"I really don't have anything to add to what I've already told you, Sam." She'd racked her brain these past couple of minutes, trying to remember some small, salient clue she could offer him that would turn out to be the crucial piece of the puzzle and solve this awful crime, but she had come up with nothing. "Celia and I were alone in the bridal room. When I left the room, she was still fussing with her veil. When I came back a few minutes later, she was exactly the way you saw her—dead on the floor."

Zoe pressed her lips together, struggling to keep her voice from breaking again. Crying wasn't going to do anyone any good, least of all Celia. "And you know the rest."

"You forgot a part," Sam told her, his voice neither accusing, nor annoyed. He was merely calling her attention to a fact.

She looked at Sam quizzically. She'd told him everything. "What?"

He leaned in a little closer over the desk, creating a sense of intimacy. He was well aware of the fact that trust was grounded in intimacy. "You said you argued with Celia."

She'd forgotten about telling him that for a second. Or maybe she'd just pushed it out of her mind. Either way, it wasn't something she was willing to bring out into the light of day. Besides, the argument had no bearing on her death.

"Oh. Yes." That whole episode came rushing back to her. "We did."

"What was the argument about?" he asked her pointedly, watching her carefully.

Sam's voice was even more authoritative than usual. Ordinarily, she would have already volunteered the subject matter of the argument. It had always been in her nature to be as helpful as possible. But in this particular instance, nothing had changed about the way she felt regarding the argument.

She couldn't tell Sam what Celia had told her. Knowing would only hurt Sam and it would serve no purpose to tell him now. It certainly had no bearing on Celia's murder.

Raising her head like someone defiantly guarding a secret, Zoe answered, "It's private."

"There's nothing private about a murder," Sam informed her.

She stared at the man she had loved for as long as she could remember, trying to make sense of what he had just told her. Holding stubbornly onto her convictions, she brazened it out.

"The argument had nothing to do with Celia's death. I didn't kill my sister, if that's what you're leading up to. Why would I?" she challenged.

This was an entirely different Zoe than he had ever seen before. He wondered if it was just the stress of the situation, or if there was another reason for the change in her behavior. Could it have something to do with the plain Jane suddenly coming out from beneath her far more vivacious sister's shadow?

"I don't know," Sam answered. "You tell me."

"I *am* telling you—I didn't do it. I'll do everything I can to help you find whoever murdered my sister—but it wasn't me," Zoe insisted.

Sam said nothing for a long moment, choosing instead to study her in silence.

After what seemed like an eternity to Zoe, he finally told her, "I believe you. But don't leave town. I may have more questions for you."

"Where would I go?" she asked him simply. "Granite Gulch is my home."

Sam merely nodded in absent acknowledgment, his mind already elsewhere.

Whether the red dot was off center or not, the red bull's-eye on Celia's forehead was too reminiscent of his father's signature trademark not to have something to do with Matthew Colton in some way.

But what?

Since his father most definitely was in prison, this had to be the work of a copycat killer. But if so, to what end? Why would this killer choose to follow in the old man's footsteps, but deliberately elect to ignore the fact that Matthew killed middle-aged men? Why had he killed a young woman in her twenties?

"Zoe," Sam said as she began to rise from her seat.

Zoe was on her feet, but her hands remained on the armrests, as if she expected him to tell her to sit down again. "Yes?"

"Did you see anyone hanging around the bridal room when you left or when you were coming back?" Maybe she had seen the killer and hadn't realized it.

But Zoe shook her head. She'd already asked herself the same question several times, trying to conjure up someone in the shadows. But she always came up empty. She hadn't seen anyone.

"Everyone was in the church, waiting for the ceremony to start," she told Sam.

"Well, there had to be *someone*," he said, talking more to himself than to Zoe. "Celia didn't just shoot herself—the angle's wrong," he added almost matter-of-factly, as if arguing the fact in front of a board of inquiry.

Since he'd already dismissed her, Zoe left the shelter of the chair. But she felt she needed to say something before she walked out of the room. Celia's motive for tricking Sam into marrying her had been clear. Celia had loved money and she'd wanted to live the high life. The Coltons, once pariahs because of their father, were once more a wealthy family and had been accepted back into the community's good graces.

As far as she could ascertain, Sam was marrying Celia to give the unborn child he thought was coming a name. But maybe somewhere within all that noble behavior, he had actually loved her sister. For that reason, she offered him her condolences, even though the words were somewhat hackneyed.

"I'm sorry for your loss, Sam," Zoe told him softly.

Sam's expression never changed. She might as well have said it looked like it might rain later. But he went through the obligatory motions and said, "Yeah, same here," because, after all, she had lost a sister, and that loss undoubtedly meant more to her than his losing his wife-to-be did to him.

What he did regret, far more than he'd ever thought he would, was that he had lost his unborn child in all of this.

Zoe offered him a small, rather sad smile and said "Thank you," just before she left the room.

Sam rose to his feet a moment later. There was still a church full of people to question and he sincerely doubted the backup crew he'd called in had managed to make more than a small dent in that crowd.

Leaving the reverend's office, he started to go down the hall and back to the church, only to run into Trevor. His oldest brother had been invited to the wedding along with their other siblings and at first, Sam thought Trevor was looking for him to offer his condolences, just like Zoe had.

But one look at the FBI profiler's grim expression told him that wasn't the reason why Trevor was looking for him.

"Good. I found you. I just got a look at the victim," Trevor said, not bothering to offer any perfunctory niceties first.

His brother stopped directly in front of him, blocking his path back to the church. It was obvious Trevor wanted to talk to him away from the others, even though they were both law enforcement agents.

This was, in part, a family matter and not a conversation either one of them would want overheard by just anyone.

"And?" Sam asked, waiting for the rest of it, because there was obviously a "rest of it."

Trevor frowned, as if saying the words actually caused him pain. "Your fiancée fits a new emerging pattern."

For there to be a "new emerging pattern," there had to be more. "Go on," Sam urged quietly.

Trevor gave him a quick summary of the details that he had. "In the past two months, two young women, both in their twenties with long dark hair, were found murdered in Blackthorn County. Each of them had a red bull's-eye drawn on their forehead. And, in each case, the red dot was just slightly off center, same as your fiancée. Now here's the really weird part—"

"Right, because the rest of what you just said isn't weird at all," Sam commented sarcastically.

His own world had ceased being normal the day his father had murdered his mother, but this seemingly baseless murder was hard for even him to come to terms with.

Trevor continued as if his younger brother hadn't said anything. Given the shock Sam had just received, minutes away from taking his wedding vows, Trevor felt that under the circumstances, his brother could be given a great deal of leeway.

Trevor continued with his narrative. "The first victim's name started with the letter *A*, and the second victim's name began with *B*. And your fiancée's name began with—"

"The letter *C*," Sam concluded. His eyes never left his brother's as he tried to put the facts into some kind of coherent order. "So what are you saying, that this was all premeditated? That the killer is playing some kind of a sick game, copying his murders after another serial killer, then adding his own sick twist to it?"

Trevor nodded. "Yeah, weird though it is, that's what it's beginning to look like," he confirmed. "Up until now, it was only speculation on our part. Two similar murders makes for a coincidence. Three similar murders makes it a pattern, and," he added, "it also throws these crimes into the realm of the murderer being a serial killer."

Sam paused, trying to assimilate this latest information he'd been given.

"So it's not just murdering when the urge hits him, killing women who just happen to fit a certain 'type,' the way Matthew did with his nine victims of choice. This killer had to know his victims ahead of time in order to stick to *his* pattern of choice."

Feeling momentarily oppressed and weary, Sam looked at his oldest brother. "How did the world get to be so screwed up?"

"Not the world, Sam," Trevor told him. "Just certain bad seeds in it. And to answer your question, I think it's always been like this to a certain extent."

About to say something else, Trevor paused instead, searching for words to express his sentiments. Words didn't seem to come easy to any of them in the family, he thought ruefully.

Still, he knew he had to give it his best shot. "Look, Sam, I'm sorry about your fiancée—" he began.

Unwilling to watch Trevor struggle needlessly, Sam waved his hand at his brother's attempts to express his regrets.

"Yeah, I know." And then, in a far firmer voice, he told Trevor, "Let's just get this SOB and make sure he doesn't kill anyone else."

Trevor couldn't have agreed with him more. "Amen to that."

Just then, a thought occurred to Sam. "You think he has a list?" he asked his brother.

Trevor looked at him quizzically. "What do you mean?"

"A list of names," Sam specified. "You know, women he's interacted with or maybe just stalked for a while. Women who fit that rather run-of-the-mill description that seems to set him off for some reason. He finds out their names, writes them down, then alphabetizes them so he can eliminate them in order. All that takes time, planning," he pointed out.

"Who knows what he thinks," Trevor countered. "But that would seem like the logical way to proceed," he granted, and then laughed. It was a hollow, almost sad sound.

"What's so funny?" Sam wanted to know. The whole situation was the complete opposite of funny as far as he was concerned.

"A logical serial killer," Trevor answered. "It's not funny, really. More like absurd," he corrected.

"Not to the victims," Sam commented.

For a moment, Trevor realized he'd forgotten how very personal the last murder was. He hadn't meant to sound so insensitive about the woman who would have been Sam's wife by now if she hadn't been murdered.

"Sorry," he apologized. "I meant no offense."

"None taken," Sam assured him.

He felt almost guilty at his lack of grief over Celia's death. Everyone was treating him with kid gloves, assuming he was stoically bearing up to this tragic blow. He just didn't feel right about deceiving them this way.

But this wasn't the time to come right out and admit he had no feelings for the woman, that all there had been was a sense of obligation, nothing more, behind the wedding.

He had no time to deal with that right now, Sam told himself. There was a killer to catch.

He thought for a moment, then asked abruptly, "Why women with long dark hair?"

Caught off guard, Trevor shook his head. "No idea," he confessed.

"Maybe we can find the answer with the first victim. Victim A," Sam clarified. But even as he said it, another idea had hit him. "If that actually *was* his first victim."

Trevor wasn't following him. "What do you mean?" he asked.

Sam was extrapolating as he went, building on his initial idea. "Maybe our serial killer killed someone before that, someone the police didn't find. The person our killer actually hated," he specified. "The person all the other victims remind him of."

"Okay," Trevor agreed. "But why kill these others alphabetically?" In his opinion, that ramped the murders up another notch, making them that much more difficult to execute.

Sam thought for a moment, and then he shrugged. "Maybe our killer is an obsessive-compulsive type and whatever makes those birds tick makes him want to conduct these killings in this specific, macabre, alphabetical fashion."

It was, Trevor thought, as good a theory as any—and better than most.

"You know," he told Sam, "if you ever decide you want to move up from being a detective in a town the size of a green pea, the FBI Behavioral Bureau could use someone like you."

Sam knew he should be flattered by the invitation, but all he really was…was numb. But, this was his brother, and relations were still in the very early reacquaintance stages, so he proceeded as if he was crossing a river in a skiff made of eggshells.

"Thanks, but no thanks. Two serial killers in one lifetime is more than enough for me," he assured his oldest brother.

They both knew he was referring to their father as well as to the current killer who had suddenly raised his head and thrown everything into chaos.

About to return to the church and the remaining wedding guests that still needed to give their statements, Sam turned to his brother with another, more pressing thought. "You know, before we go on with this investigation, given what's already happened, I think we should release this story to the local papers."

Trevor looked at him as if he'd lost his mind. "The papers? What the hell for? Those reporters are nothing more than vultures. At the very least, they'll just get in the way."

He probably hated reporters more than Trevor did, or at least equally as much. When the story had broken about their father, the reporters had had a field day, camping on their front lawn, following them everywhere and always, always snapping pictures and shouting out embarrassing, humiliating questions.

But there was a reason for his break with protocol. "I'd be the first to agree with you," Sam said, "but since this nutjob has already killed three women that fit a certain description and pattern, it stands to reason that his next victim will be a twentysomething, dark-haired woman whose name begins with the letter *D*.

"It seems only right that we issue a warning so these women will exercise extreme caution and do what it takes to stay out of harm's way. Otherwise, if this maniac kills a fourth victim, her death will be as much on our heads as on his."

Trevor sighed. "I wouldn't exactly say fifty-fifty, but you've got a point. You want to release a formal statement to the press?"

Sam was stunned by his brother's suggestion. He had a tendency to clam up in front of a microphone. Press conferences weren't his calling.

"Me? Hell no. We've got someone in charge of PR at the station to do that." The name of the woman escaped him at the moment. "If they have me talking to the news media, public relations between the police and the press will plummet down below sea level. Maybe even lower."

"Haven't lost that charming touch of yours, have you?" Trevor laughed.

"No occasion to," Sam answered and it seemed to Trevor that his younger brother wasn't really kidding.

Walking into the church proper again, Sam saw the wedding guests were growing somewhat restless as they sat in the pews. He assumed a number of them had been interviewed by now, but everyone was being detained until the last statement was taken.

Sam looked around for Annabel, the person he had temporarily put in charge of this phase. Spotting her, he called his sister over to him.

Annabel was wearing a light blue cocktail dress and looked less like a police officer than usual. At the moment, she was in the middle of questioning one of the wedding guests. She paused when she saw Sam waving her over.

"Be right back," she said to the older woman, patting her hand. With that, she made her way over to her brother. The first word out of her mouth was, "Anything?"

"I was going to ask you the same thing."

Annabel was a great deal more loquacious than he was and she had the ability to get people to talk to her. He felt certain that if any of these people had the slightest inclination to talk and "share secrets" they would do it with Annabel.

"Nobody saw anything," Annabel replied needlessly. She did it to ensure the fact that her brother wouldn't think she was hiding something from him.

"Didn't think so, but it was still worth a shot. Have all the statements on my desk when you and the others get finished." That simple act, he thought, assured him of eyestrain and a headache the size of a medium boulder.

"You got it." There was a pause before she said, "And, Sam—"

He was developing a sixth sense about this. He knew what she was going to say before she had a chance to say it.

"Yeah, I know. You want to tell me that you're very sorry for my loss." He forced a smile to his lips. "Thanks."

Annabel hesitated for a moment, debating saying anything at all. Sam was obviously steeling himself off from the events, reacting to it only as a police detective, not as anything else. But remaining silent on the subject didn't really sit all that well with her.

"You know, you could try to look a little more broken up, all things considered," she suggested.

"It's all on the inside, Annabel," he replied. "I don't believe in putting on a show for anyone."

"I know that, but other people don't know you as well as the guys and I do," his sister pointed out, referring to their other siblings.

Sam shrugged. "Other people don't count," he replied and, to a good extent, he meant it.

Chapter 4

Sam hadn't gotten very far with questioning the remaining wedding guests when he heard a commotion directly behind him.

Turning toward the sound, he saw Zoe and several men—waiters, judging from the uniforms they had on—entering the rear of the church. The waiters were pushing carts before them laden with appetizers and soft drinks. In the center of both carts were platters of sliced roast beef. A third cart brought up the rear. It was filled with plates, glasses and utensils.

"What the hell's going on here?" Sam demanded, looking squarely at Zoe since she was the one who seemed to be leading this parade. "I thought I told you to go home."

Zoe paused in front of him, but rather than answer his question, she gave the waiters instructions first. "You can set up right in front of the first pew," she told the two waiters next to her. "If it's all right with you, Reverend," she added, looking at the somewhat bemused preacher.

"Who am I to stand in the way of feeding the masses?" he asked with a slight chuckle.

Trying to hold his impatience in check, Sam shifted so he was directly in Zoe's line of vision. "What are you doing?" he demanded.

Zoe wasn't accustomed to acting on her own initiative, but after everything that had happened today, she felt obligated to bring some sort of small order to all the ensuing chaos. She knew she wasn't going to be much help when it came to finding out who had killed Celia, but she could at least feed the people who were involved in this investigation, be it the wedding guests who were being questioned, or the law enforcement agents who were doing the questioning.

"I thought maybe the wedding guests might be better able to answer your questions if they ate something. The food's all paid for," she explained quickly, "and it seemed a shame just to let it all go to waste like that. Besides, people tend to be more mellow on a full stomach."

She was right, but, while he didn't want to starve anyone, in his opinion bringing food into the equation somehow trivialized the murder.

"This isn't some backyard barbecue, Zoe," he reminded Zoe.

The smile she had deliberately been forcing herself to wear faded away as her eyes met his.

"Yes, I know that. It's my sister's wedding day—

except she didn't get a chance to get married. Someone callously took her life and robbed her of that. Maybe this is my way of coping with that knowledge, by making things a little more tolerable for the people who, through no fault of their own, suddenly find themselves part of a crime scene."

Zoe had too good a heart for what was happening here, Sam thought. People with good hearts inevitably wound up getting hurt.

"One of them might have done it, you know," he pointed out.

"I know," she acknowledged quietly. "But then again, she might have been murdered by a complete stranger."

"How would he have gotten past everyone unnoticed?" Sam challenged.

Zoe threw up her hands. "I don't know. But I'm not going to punish the others because the murderer might be hiding in their midst. Hopefully, whoever he is, if he is mingling here, will choke on the food." She paused, scrutinizing Sam. He looked drawn, like a man going through hell. "Maybe you should eat something, too," she suggested. "Besides everything else, you *are* the one who footed the bill."

Her comment caught him by surprise. He hadn't wanted any of that to come out and get around. What he paid for was his business.

"What makes you say that?" he asked defensively.

"Because it's the truth," she replied simply. "Celia bragged to me about it. That she got you to pay for the whole wedding, including her dress. And even if she hadn't said anything, Celia was my sister. I know she didn't have the kind of money that would have paid for the wedding she felt she was entitled to." Zoe paused for another moment before adding, "She bragged to me about that, too, that she got you to pay for exactly what she wanted."

Celia had been her sister and she wouldn't have had this sort of fate befall Celia for the world, but Sam deserved better than that—especially now that she knew Celia had tricked him into agreeing to marry her.

Putting her hand on his shoulder, Zoe said gently, "I'm sure no one'll fault you for taking a break to eat something."

She glanced toward the front of the church, where she'd told the waiters to set up. Almost all the pews had been emptied out or were in the process of emptying, with all the people filing by the carts that had been placed next to one another.

"Provided, of course," she observed, "that they let you cut in line."

"I don't have an appetite," Sam replied flatly.

That didn't seem to be anyone else's problem, Zoe thought, watching the wedding guests fill their plates. But as for her, she understood perfectly what Sam was saying.

"Funny, neither do I," she confided. She hadn't eaten this morning—there just hadn't seemed to be enough time—and after finding Celia's body, her stomach was so tightly knotted, there was no way she would be able to get a single spoonful of anything down today. Maybe not even tomorrow.

Barely acknowledging what she'd just said, Sam began to head over to the wedding guests to continue taking down their statements when he stopped to glance back at Zoe one last time.

She was standing quietly on the perimeter of the gathering, silently observing everyone else gratefully helping themselves to the food that would have been served at the reception.

At *his* wedding reception.

He knew he should be feeling a whole host of emotions about that, but the truth of it was, he felt nothing. Not anger at Celia's untimely death, not fury he'd been cheated out of experiencing a more normal lifestyle than he'd had so far. If anything, the one thing he did feel cheated of was that he was never going to be able to hold his child in his arms. He'd never be able to look down on his or her face.

But even that, Sam told himself, might have actually turned out for the best. Any child born these days had a great many things to overcome before he or she became an adult. He knew from firsthand experience kids didn't always reach that stage relatively intact. Maybe it was better his child would never have to go through and endure those kinds of conditions, Sam told himself.

For now, he shook himself free of that morose

thought. Catching Zoe's attention, he suggested, "I can have one of the uniforms bring you home."

Zoe shook her head. "Thanks, but I'm really not ready to be alone right now. I thought I'd just stick around here and help out with the food, or whatever else might come up and need doing," she told him.

Then, not wanting to get in Sam's way or to be the cause of any further concern for him, she went up to the front of the church and offered to provide an extra set of hands. She knew that getting the guests fed would go even faster that way.

Taking down statements, even when the person being questioned had nothing really concrete to offer, took longer than Sam had expected. Although those guests who were being questioned had nothing in the way of real evidence to contribute, it seemed they all wanted to offer either a theory regarding the murder or an opinion as to why it had happened, not to mention awkwardly stumbling through condolences they felt obligated to offer the would-be bridegroom.

Few of them had ever been this close to a murder and they were all apparently repelled and yet fascinated by the circumstances at the same time.

For his part, Sam cut off the more long-winded guests once they were wound up. But he did listen to each of them, thinking there just might be some sort of a clue to be found tangled up in all their verbal ramblings.

In the end, after taking the last statement from a

sweet-faced older woman named Abigail Abernathy, Sam was forced to admit he had nothing. No motive for the murder had become apparent, no suspicious behavior was noted by anyone. He was no further along after more than three hours of taking down statements than he had been immediately after he had discovered Zoe screaming in the bridal room.

Frustrated, he knew what his next logical step had to be—which only added to his overall frustration.

Since the way the murder had been conducted was so similar to the way his father had killed his nine victims, Sam felt some of the answers he was looking for could very well be found with his father.

Which meant he needed to travel to the prison where his father was incarcerated and question the man. By no stretch of the imagination was that something he felt like doing. It had been nearly twenty years since he had seen Matthew Colton—the exact length of time since the man had been sent to prison for his crimes.

As far as Sam was concerned, another twenty could go by without a visit, as well.

But he owed it to Celia—as well as to his unborn child and the other two victims that had been uncovered—to find out who killed her. And right now, he had a very uneasy feeling that the killer was most likely a devoted disciple of his father's. Some worshipful fanatic who wanted to be just like Matthew Colton, God help them.

The world, he thought, not for the first time, was a very strange, unsettling place.

Sam looked around the church. Now that he had made up his mind to see Matthew and discover what sort of information he could get out of the man, he was eager to get this whole thing over with and behind him.

But nothing would get done today. It was getting late. Visiting hours at the prison were over and he wouldn't endear himself to anyone by flashing his badge and demanding rules be broken for him so he could question his sociopathic father.

He needed time to psyche himself up mentally before actually confronting the old man. Besides, the first thing he needed was to sleep. That was, of course, assuming he could actually get some sleep, something that at this point he sincerely doubted.

"Everyone," Sam said, raising his voice and waiting until he had the wedding guests' attention. When he did, he proceeded. "Thank you for your statements and your patience," he told the collective gathering. "You're all free to leave. If any of you remember anything that might have slipped your minds while giving your accounts of this morning, you were all given cards with the number of the police department on them. Please don't hesitate to call me or one of the other police detectives."

Standing off to the side, Sam watched as the guests began to file by and make their way through the double doors to the outside world.

Within minutes, the room was quickly cleared, leaving only a handful of police personnel in their wake.

The latter group left soon enough, either heading back to the police station, or in some cases, home for the night.

That was when he realized Zoe was still there. She was helping the waiters clear away the last of the remaining food. One of the waiters was putting what was left into a couple of large boxes that had been used to transport the sliced wedding cake.

Once all the food had been boxed up, Zoe turned the leftovers over to the reverend, saying, "I'm sure there're some deserving families in Granite Gulch who might enjoy these leftovers."

"Indeed there are," Reverend Rimmer told her with a grateful smile. And then the smile turned sympathetic as he asked her, concerned, "Will you be all right tonight, Zoe?"

"I'll be fine, Reverend. I already *am* fine. Thank you for asking," she told him, turning away.

"You know, it's not right to lie to a reverend," Sam told her, moving out of the shadows where he had stood observing her these past few minutes.

Zoe stifled a gasp of surprise. Recovering herself, she insisted proudly, "I wasn't lying."

"Oh?" It was obvious by his tone he didn't believe her.

Zoe raised her chin in almost a defiant stance, something she wasn't accustomed to. "No," she maintained stubbornly. "I wasn't lying. I was setting his mind at ease."

So that was what they called it these days, he thought sarcastically. Out loud he challenged, "And there's a difference?"

"There is for him," she informed Sam. And then she shrugged. "There's no point in making him feel he has to find a way to comfort me." Her voice dropped to almost a whisper as she continued, "Besides, right now, there is no way to comfort me and probably won't be for quite some time to come."

He knew what she was dealing with. He had gone through the same thing when his mother had been killed. "Every day it gets a little easier to deal with. It never gets easy," he warned, "but it does eventually get easier."

Except for the times when the nightmares bring it all back in vivid colors, he thought. That was the sort of thing that sent a person back to square one. But Zoe didn't need to know that right now. She would find herself dealing with all of it soon enough, at least that was his guess.

She was grateful to Sam for trying to make this easier for her. She was well aware it wasn't really in his nature to connect to people.

"Was it that way for you?" she asked him.

He didn't answer her, didn't want to make this any more personal than he had to. That wasn't his way and even if he would have wanted to—and he didn't—making any kind of a real personal connection was next to impossible for him. Because of what had happened in his childhood, he was emotionally stunted. He'd spent too many years disciplining himself to keep his distance from people, both physically and emotionally, because to do otherwise was just asking for pain.

He'd succeeded all too well.

Still, he couldn't just walk away and leave Zoe here in this condition. Zoe looked too much like a lost waif for him to just ignore and forget about her. Besides, had things gone on schedule—instead of so horribly wrong—by now Zoe would have been his sister-in-law, which made her family. And family was always taken care of, regardless of any feelings that might or might not have been involved.

"Get your things, Zoe," he instructed. "I'm taking you home."

"That's all right. You don't have to," she said almost automatically.

She didn't feel right about taking Sam away from his duties. Celia had tricked him and she felt somehow obligated to make it up to Sam. Turning him into a personal chauffeur was not paying the man back in any manner, shape or form.

Sam exhaled impatiently. He was not about to argue with her about this. He was driving her home, which meant she was coming with him, no questions asked.

"I don't like repeating myself, Zoe. Consider this

the one and only exception. Get your things, I'm taking you home."

Zoe looked at him hesitantly, as if she wanted to say something to him, but couldn't find the courage or the words.

"What?" he demanded impatiently.

"They're in the bridal room. My things," she further clarified uneasily.

"That makes them part of the crime scene." But he didn't recall seeing anything like a purse or her street clothing in the room. "Were they out in plain sight?" he questioned.

"No, I put them in the closet. I didn't want them getting in Celia's way," she explained.

It all seemed so petty, so terribly insignificant now, she thought. Celia had been immersed in playing the queen, having her smallest wish obeyed.

All Sam had heard was that the things were in a closet. That meant there was a chance the items hadn't been tagged and taken.

With that in mind, Sam started out the double doors. "C'mon," he urged.

Without looking to see if she was following, Sam led the way back to the room where her sister had been murdered.

Zoe was right behind him.

She stopped short when she saw there was yellow tape across the doorway. Zoe hesitated, looking from the tape to Sam.

"Doesn't this mean we shouldn't cross it?"

"It means that no *unauthorized* personnel should cross it. I'm not unauthorized," he informed her, raising the tape. When she made no effort to move, he asked her, "Well, what are you waiting for, a special invitation?"

"No. Sorry." Apologizing, she hurried under the yellow tape, then went straight to the closet, where she stopped. "Can I open it?"

"Is that what you did when you put your things away?" he asked.

It was a rhetorical question, but she answered it as if he meant it seriously. "Yes."

"Then open it now. Your prints are already on the doorknob."

She carefully did as Sam instructed, taking out both her purse—a small clutch thing, he noted—and her street dress.

Now that he thought about it, she had always dressed so simply, Sam recalled. Clothes that made her fade into the woodwork. But on closer scrutiny, he realized she was like a hidden diamond, just waiting to catch the right light. Or, in Zoe's case, it was her inner peace that just radiated outward upon inspection.

"So, is that everything?" he asked her, nodding at what she had in her hands.

Zoe nodded solemnly, not wanting to delay him a second longer than she had to. "Yes."

"Then let's go," he ordered.

Wanting to protest, Zoe remained silent. She

waited until she walked out again, ducking beneath the yellow tape as he held it up for her.

Once she was out of the room, she turned toward Sam abruptly and gave it one more try. "You really don't have to take me home, you know. I can call someone," she volunteered.

"In case you haven't noticed, I'm 'someone.' Now stop arguing with me or you're going to be riding home with a gag across your mouth. Understand?"

"Understand," she echoed. She doubted he would carry out his threat, but she wasn't a hundred percent sure of that.

"Good," he said with finality just before he led the way to the parking lot.

Chapter 5

The silence inside his car felt oddly disturbing to Sam.

In general, he wasn't much for small talk—or any sort of talk actually, if he could avoid it. For the most part, he let others do the talking if they wanted to and he listened when he had to. Or when there was something to be gleaned from whatever it was that the other person was saying. He had already figured out Zoe couldn't be classified as a chatterbox—that title had belonged to Celia and his guess was that growing up, Zoe had learned to keep her own counsel and allow Celia to take the center stage.

Silences were usually welcomed by him. But there was something a bit uncomfortable about this one.

He could sense Zoe's inner struggle, sense her trying to come to terms with what had happened today. While he had no words of comfort to offer her—comforting the grieving was a skill he had never quite managed to develop—he knew there were times when just talking helped.

Not that it would have helped him, but his was not an average case and he had long since accepted he was not the average person.

Zoe, he figured, was.

"How are you holding up?" he finally asked as he turned into a residential development.

She didn't want to talk about her feelings, didn't even want to think about them, really. In an uncustomary reaction, she turned the tables on him and said, "I could ask you the same thing."

Sam laughed shortly. "Yeah, but I asked you first," he pointed out.

She blew out a breath and realized, too late, it was a shaky one. She was supposed to be in control here, not falling apart, Zoe upbraided herself. She didn't want Sam thinking she was angling for pity.

"I'm fine," she answered almost stoically.

He slanted a glance at her. Even a quick look told him she was in bad shape—and sinking fast. "No, you're not."

"Okay, I'm not," she admitted, knowing there was no sense in trying to lie to Sam. She wasn't that good at it. "But I will be—given time."

"Yes, you will," he agreed.

He wanted to leave it there, but he knew he couldn't. Zoe wasn't like him. She didn't have an iron shell around her to protect her from things like this. Zoe *felt* things, he thought, felt things he knew he couldn't.

"Do you want me to call someone?" he offered. "When I drop you off at your place, do you want me to call someone?" He caught her confused expression out of the corner of his eye. "To have them come over and stay with you." he explained further.

Zoe shook her head. She couldn't think of a single person she wanted to have stay with her—except for him, and she wasn't about to ask him, so that left no one.

"There's no one to call," she told him. "Not about this. I can't exactly say, 'Somebody killed Celia. Can you come over and hold my hand?'"

Her wording struck him as telling. "Do you want that?" he asked her, curious. "To have someone hold your hand?"

Oh, God, did he think she was making a veiled request? Zoe shook her head adamantly. "No. It's just a figure of speech."

Sam pulled up in front of her house. Parking his vehicle at the curb, he surprised Zoe by getting out and crossing around to her side. She'd already opened the passenger door. He opened it wider, then took her hand and helped her out.

She had no idea why the touch of his hand would affect her the way it did. Until that moment, after she'd managed to regain her composure in the bridal room, she had exercised immense self-control, holding herself together and putting on a brave front.

But there was something about making human contact—just an innocent touching of hands—that suddenly sliced through everything. Zoe could feel herself instantly crumbling inside.

She struggled hard against showing anything, but she couldn't seem to keep the tears from coming to her eyes. Within seconds, the facade she had managed to bravely construct was being betrayed.

Sam felt completely at a loss. He had no idea how to react in the face of tears. When he came right down to it, he would rather have faced down a gun-wielding criminal or subdued an angry, foul-mouth agitator. He was equipped for that, trained for that. He knew how to handle himself in those sorts of situations.

But tears? Who the hell knew what to do with a crying female? Especially since *this* female wasn't carrying on. Zoe actually looked as if she was as embarrassed to be shedding her tears as he was embarrassed to be witnessing them.

Digging into his back pocket, he pulled out his handkerchief—carrying one had been an engrained habit he'd picked up long ago, thanks to his mother's instruction—and handed it to Zoe.

"Here," he muttered, barely audible.

Taking the handkerchief from him, Zoe wiped her eyes carefully. "Sorry," she murmured. Finished, she offered it back to him.

"Hang on to it," he told her. "You might need it later."

She nodded, unable to offer an argument at the moment, unable to speak, really, without being afraid a sob might escape.

Taking out her key, she unlocked her door. When she turned around to thank him and say good-night, she found he was right behind her.

"You're blocking the doorway. Go inside," he told her.

She remained where she was, looking up at him quizzically.

"The others can handle the initial paperwork," he told her, referring to Annabel and the officers from the precinct who had responded to his call for backup. "I'll stay here for a while."

Her response to that was more tears. "I can't seem to make them stop," she apologized.

He found himself enfolding her in his arms. Because of the situation, it began awkwardly, but he managed to get himself to relax and the tension slipped away.

Having his arms around her felt like heaven, but it also felt deceitful somehow. Zoe struggled for a second time to regain control. She didn't want him to think she was using tears to make him stay with her. Those were Celia's tricks. She didn't play tricks.

Taking a step back, Zoe stumbled through an apology. "I don't want to impose—"

Zoe was not conforming to what little he knew about women. "Will you stop being so damn noble for a few minutes? Cry, rant, scream—although maybe not as loud as you did before," he qualified. "You're entitled," he told her. "She was your sister."

He was being kind to her and it was that kindness

that was undoing her, weakening her resolve to be strong. She did her best to sound blasé.

"This isn't exactly the way you expected to spend tonight, either, is it?"

Sam never liked focusing on himself. He liked other people doing it even less.

"Never mind me," he told her. "I want to make sure you're all right." And she wasn't. No matter what she maintained to the contrary, he could see she wasn't. "Are you sure there's no one you want me to call for you?"

She offered him a smile. It was a weak effort at best. "No. Thanks."

Sam shrugged. He sure as hell wasn't leaving her like this. Who knew what she might do in her present state of mind? He wasn't about to have Zoe on his conscience along with all the other things that haunted it.

"Then I guess I'll stay for a while," he told her.

She didn't want him feeling obligated to her, or worse, manipulated by her to stay. "But—"

He held his hand up. Sam had no desire to repeat this dance again. They'd only wind up going around in circles—something that, by definition, always irritated him.

"I don't want you to be alone," he informed her. "So, since there's no one you want me to call, I'll stay here for a while."

Again, although she was grateful for his thoughtfulness and just his very presence, which went a long way to making her feel better, Zoe felt obligated to point out the obvious.

"You can't babysit me. You have a case to solve."

Sam looked at her in silence for a long moment. His eyes seemed to penetrate right down into the very core of her. "You're nothing like your sister, are you?"

Was that a criticism? Did he find her lacking? Of course he did, Zoe upbraided herself. Celia had been exciting, beautiful. She was just a mousy librarian in an awful blue dress.

"What do you mean?" she heard herself asking Sam in a small voice.

Sam felt something protective being aroused within him. It caught him completely off guard and by surprise. He hadn't actually *felt* anything in a long time, least of all protective. It reinforced his feeling about how different Zoe was from her older sister.

Celia had thrived on being the center of attention. She had demanded it most of the time and she'd been known to actually act out if she was denied that attention. Even when he'd asked her to marry him, he'd felt their life together didn't stand much of a chance of making it, given the fact that his work took him away for long stretches of time. That sort of thing put a strain on the best of relationships, and given that Celia always wanted to be the center of the universe, their marriage was pretty much doomed before it ever became a reality.

But now wasn't the time to talk about Celia's shortcomings. He and Zoe were both aware of them. He had a feeling Zoe was no stranger to that aspect of her sister, either.

"Just that you have a tendency to put others before yourself. Got any coffee?" he asked, abruptly changing the subject. It was a lot easier talking about nothing than about something, at least for him.

Zoe brightened at finally being given something to do. "Yes. I'll put on a pot." She turned toward the kitchen counter as she said it, pulling the coffeemaker closer to her.

"Why don't you change first?" Sam suggested, nodding at the bridesmaid dress she had on. In his opinion, the wide skirt made it awkward for her to move around and reach things. "That doesn't exactly look like the sort of outfit that someone should wear in the kitchen."

She looked down at the bridesmaid dress. While it wasn't the kind that could be instantly labeled as memorably hideous, it was still far from flattering, which she knew had been why her sister had chosen it to begin with. Gorgeous though she had been, Celia wanted to take no chances that anyone in the bridal party was going to be able to hold a candle to her.

"Well, it's not like I'm ever going to be wearing this again," Zoe commented. Especially since she would never be able to look at this dress and not immediately associate it with Celia's murder. "But you're right. It's not exactly made for moving around in freely."

Taking out a can of coffee from the refrigerator,

where she kept it once it was opened, she went through the motions of measuring out the right amount of coffee to prepare a fresh pot.

Measuring spoon in her hand, she raised her eyes to his. “You take it strong, right?”

“Yes—how d’you know?” he couldn’t help asking. To his recollection, they had never stopped for coffee together, nor had he ever had any in her presence.

Zoe merely smiled shyly at his question. “You just look like the type,” she answered, measuring out an extra heaping tablespoon before setting the coffeemaker to brew.

“I thought you were going to change out of that,” he said, nodding at the voluminous dress.

“I am. I just wanted to get the coffee going.” Putting the coffee container back in the refrigerator, Zoe left the room quickly.

Alone, Sam began to move about the small living room and kitchen, poking through the magazines neatly piled on her coffee table, glancing over the titles on the bindings of the neatly arranged books on her bookshelves. She had, he observed, eclectic tastes.

As he glanced around, he absently noted that Zoe was a far more fastidious housekeeper than her sister had been. Celia, he recalled, would let clothes remain wherever they happened to fall when she took them off. Her idea of cleaning was to occasionally scoop things up and then dump them all in a heap in a room that wasn’t being used.

Even he was neater than that. But then, in his case,

it came from not having very much to begin with, so each item was viewed as being precious. They were always packed up because he never knew when he would be shuttled from one foster home to another. Transfers occurred abruptly and at any time.

He'd quickly learned to husband whatever he had and to keep close track of everything because if he blinked, everything he had could easily disappear.

Zoe was back before the coffeemaker had finished its loud brewing noises. She came down wearing a pullover blouse and a pair of worn jeans. The jeans were a little tight and he caught himself staring before discipline took over.

"That was quick," he commented.

She hadn't thought of it as being particularly that. She hadn't hurried any more than usual.

"Didn't seem polite to keep you waiting around out here, especially when you're going out of your way like this."

Moving to the counter, she checked the coffee pot. It had just finished brewing, so she poured him a full cup of coffee, leaving it black. As for the one she poured for herself, she went on to dilute its inky color with a heavy amount of sweetened creamer.

"So," Sam began abruptly once she had sat down across from him at the kitchen table, "what did you and Celia fight about?"

She had just gotten herself to relax and now she stiffened again. Why was he bringing that up again? Her feelings about the answer hadn't changed. For him to know the subject of her argument with Celia would only serve to hurt him.

"You don't want to know."

"If I didn't, I wouldn't have asked—twice," he pointed out.

She did her best to stand her ground. "I already told you, what we argued about doesn't have any bearing on what happened to her."

There was something there, he could swear to it, and he wasn't about to back off until he had some answers. "Then there shouldn't be a problem telling me," he said to her.

"Sam…"

"You might as well tell me, Zoe. I'm not going to let up until you do."

He meant it, she thought. She could tell by the stubborn look in his eyes. He wanted an answer and he wasn't about to leave without it. She was stuck between the proverbial rock and hard place.

But the longer she held out, the more annoyed Sam was going to be with her. Who knew where this was going to wind up—and if he brought in someone else to compel her to talk, then that other person would wind up being a witness to his humiliation.

That was what made up her mind for her.

Zoe took in a deep breath and then started talking. "I told her I resented looking like a clown at her wedding. She got mad and said I was just going to have to live with it and it was my responsibility to be there for her."

Sam pinned her down with his penetrating look. That was much too petty to have come out of Zoe's mouth, he thought.

"What was the argument *really* about, Zoe?" It was no longer a question but a demand.

That had been her last-ditch attempt to throw him off the trail. "You don't believe me?"

"No, I don't," he said, sounding more patient than he felt. "That doesn't sound like Celia talking, it sounds more like you talking. Now, for the last time, *what was the argument about*?"

She looked at him hesitantly. "You're not going to like it."

He had already suspected as much. "There're a lot of things I don't like," he told her. "Now talk, Zoe. It's either here, to me, or at the precinct and a bunch of strangers who I promise you are not nearly as easy-going as I am."

She would have laughed if she could have, because he was serious and believed what he'd just said.

She pressed her lips together, hating to be the one to tell him. Hating having to tell him at all. She frequently wished she was better at lying.

But Celia was the one who had always been good at that, not she. She'd always been, as Celia had taunted her more than once, "Miss Goody Two-Shoes, married to the truth."

"She bragged to me about something, about deceiving someone," she blurted out when he scowled at her. "I told her she had to tell that person what she'd done and she laughed at me and absolutely refused."

"I need details, Zoe." When she said nothing, he looked at her more closely. And then it came to him. "It was about me, wasn't it?"

She looked pained as she pleaded, "Don't make me tell you, Sam."

But he wasn't moved. His insides had turned to ice. "Now, Zoe."

Zoe gritted her teeth together, as if to strain all her words through them before she said them to Sam. Anything to delay the telling for even a second longer.

But then, she had no options left. Taking a breath, she told him.

"Celia said she'd tricked you into marrying her. That she wasn't even pregnant. That you and she hadn't even made love together, she just made you think you had." When he looked at her, clearly stunned and bewildered, Zoe went on to explain, "She told me that she got you drunk that night you came over after killing that criminal, then staged it so it looked as if you'd had wild, passionate sex with her.

"In the morning, when you woke up, she told you that you'd made love with her. After that, she waited for a little while, then told you that she was pregnant. She bragged to me how she knew you'd do the right thing and marry her—and you did. Or would have," she amended.

He wanted to accuse her of lying, but that was just his pride talking. One look at Zoe's face and he knew she had told him the truth—at great cost to herself. He could see it actually physically hurt her to tell him this.

The next words out of her mouth confirmed it. "I'm sorry, Sam. I didn't want to tell you," she cried, clearly distressed.

He didn't want her pity. He didn't want anything at all from her. From anyone. He just wanted to get out of there before his self-control cracked.

"I'll send Annabel over," he told her as he walked out, slamming the door behind him.

Zoe could swear she felt the vibrations of the door resounding in her chest. Somehow, it made her heart ache even more. She shouldn't have given in so easily, shouldn't have told him, or better yet, should have learned how to lie better. But lying had never been her thing.

Neither had hurting people. Least of all someone she cared about.

"I didn't want to tell you!" she called out after Sam, but her words just seemed to bounce against the closed door.

Sam couldn't hear her.

Sam was gone.

Chapter 6

Two days later found Sam sitting at his desk in the precinct, feeling more dead than alive. Sleep had, for the most part, eluded him and the hours all seemed to bleed into one another.

If it hadn't been for the department's calendar on his desk, he wouldn't have known what day it was.

His eyes growing progressively more blurry, Sam scrubbed his hands over his face. He caught himself wishing he could somehow scrub them over his mind and his waning energy level, as well, to somehow restore them to their former full running capacity.

After having managed to get—and use up—his second and then third wind, at this point he was beginning to feel like one of the living dead.

Leaning back in his chair, he felt the lump in his back pocket and remembered he'd been forced to shut off his cell phone. Somehow, reporters had managed to get his personal number and thought nothing of calling him at all hours of the day and night. After a while, it had begun to drive him crazy, which was when he'd decided to shut it off.

The phone on his desk rang as well, but those calls were usually from the general public, private citizens who claimed to have important information on the man the press had—running with what little input it did have—whimsically dubbed the Alphabet Killer.

If he believed even half the incoming calls, sightings had been made everywhere. It was amazing how one person—presumably a man, although Sam was ruling nothing out—could be in so many different places at the very same time.

Still, bizarre or not, all the calls had to be checked out. Given the limited number of people on the force, everyone now had a backlog of places to check out and callers to interview.

Still, there was nothing else currently going on in the county that came close to this kind of importance, so all the department's energy was focused on following up every clue, every shred of possible evidence. The reasoning was that the killer had to be somewhere and he had to be stopped. Since the killer wasn't invisible, someone had to have seen him, which was why every call had to be checked into.

"Sam. Hey, Sam."

Only extreme self-control kept Sam from jumping when he felt the hand on his shoulder.

Swinging around in his chair, he was ready to

spring into a defensive mode only to see the man with his hand on his shoulder was his older brother, Trevor.

The first thing Sam thought was that the FBI had a lead. But he refrained from asking, waiting for Trevor to state his business himself.

"Sorry, man, I didn't mean to startle you, but I did call your name. Where were you?" Trevor wanted to know, peering into his brother's face.

Sam said the first thing that came to mind, not wanting to admit he'd taken a momentary mental break because he was bordering on exhaustion.

"I was going over pictures of the crime scene," Sam said, nodding at the photographs on his desk.

"Damn, I don't know how you do it. If that were my fiancée who was murdered, it would be tearing me up inside," Trevor confessed. "By the way, I called your cell phone to let you know I was coming by, but it went straight to voice mail."

"I shut off the phone," Sam explained. "The vultures from the press were having a feeding frenzy. I figured if I had to say 'no comment' one more time, I couldn't be held responsible for my next action."

The lead FBI profiler laughed dryly as he dropped into the chair next to his brother's desk.

"I hear you." Trevor looked closer at his younger brother. "You look like hell, Sam. When did you last sleep? For that matter, when did you last eat?" he wanted to know, concern coming through his solemn tone.

"Did you come here to play mother?" Sam asked his brother.

So much for brotherly chit-chat, Trevor thought. He got down to business. "No, I came here to tell you in light of what's going on and all the similarities between the two cases, I took a quick trip to Oklahoma and paid Big J a visit," he told Sam, referring to their father's older brother. "I thought maybe he might have some idea if there was ever anybody who might have fantasized about copying dear old dad's MO, either back in the day, or now."

His interest aroused, for a minute Sam forgot how exhausted he was. "And?"

"And he had nothing to offer," Trevor replied, none too happily. "According to Big J—and I believe him—he hasn't seen the old man since before Matthew was sent to prison to serve out his sentence. When I talked to him, Big J seemed kind of skittish. And when I asked him what was wrong, he finally told me that he didn't want to go down on record as even having talked to me about his younger brother. I think he's afraid of retaliation by Matthew's followers.

"Or maybe," Trevor continued, "if there *is* some new copycat serial killer out there, the new guy might feel he has to kill anyone who badmouths the original serial killer." Trevor replayed his own words in his mind and shook his head. "Sounds crazy, doesn't it?" he asked, mocking himself.

If only.

"Not when it comes to the old man," Sam replied. "At this point, I'd believe anything's possible."

He stared darkly at the corner of the paper peering out from beneath the photographs he'd spread out on his desk. The report he'd just read when Trevor had walked into the room. The report was from the medical examiner's office.

It had managed, if anything, to put him into an even darker mood than he'd already found himself in.

Because the report had, indirectly, labeled him a fool.

For the moment, Sam pushed the paper back underneath the photographs, telling himself he'd deal with what was there later.

When he raised his eyes, he saw Trevor was looking at him. Dark eyes met even darker ones.

"Seriously, man, you should get some rest and something to eat," Trevor advised.

"Later," Sam said dismissively. He'd take care of his physical needs later. Right now, taking care of this was far more important. "You think this'll ever be behind us?" he asked Trevor out of the blue. "This crime spree the old man conducted?"

"It *was* behind us," Trevor pointed out, then added, "People started to forget. They started to trust us again," he recalled. "Look at our family. We got back together, most of us found places in some form of law enforcement—the authorities were willing to allow the past be the past. We've got to do the same," Trevor told him with emphasis.

"It's not that easy," Sam protested, curbing his annoyance.

"Yeah, it is," Trevor countered. "You just have to think positive. And eat, you've got to eat," Trevor told him, giving his face a quick, brotherly pat as he rose to his feet. "That's an order."

"I don't take orders from the FBI," Sam told his brother.

"This wasn't from the FBI," Trevor informed him. "It was from your older brother who, by the way, knows best. I'll be back to check on you," he told Sam just before he walked out.

"I'll make sure I won't be around," Sam responded, raising his voice so it would follow his brother out of the office.

Sam gave it to the count of ten, glanced back toward the doorway to make sure his brother was gone, then slipped the report out from beneath the photographs. Holding it in his hands, he looked at the autopsy report again.

He'd already read it three times and knew the words by heart.

The words confirmed the fact that he had been played for a fool.

Leaning forward, Sam took his cell phone out of his back pocket, turned it on and looked at it. A quick check of his voice mail told him he had forty-two messages. Turning his cell phone off again, he put it back into his pocket.

Selecting several of the most recent calls that had

come into the office claiming to have seen this new serial killer, he folded the papers and rose from his desk.

There was some place he needed to stop before he got back to work.

She wasn't there.

When he stopped by Zoe's place, she didn't answer the door when he rang the bell. A quick survey of the area told him that her car was gone.

As was Annabel's.

Fishing out his cell phone, he turned it on. Pressing a single number, he called his sister first. After all, he had dispatched her to spend a couple of nights with Zoe. The official reason was to make sure she remained safe and to guard Zoe in case this newly minted serial killer decided to veer from the alphabet and just go on a killing spree.

Unofficially, having Annabel stay with her was to help Zoe deal with the trauma of her sister's murder as well as being the one who had discovered the body.

If something was wrong, Annabel would have called and told him, he reasoned.

That still didn't calm his nerves.

"Where are you?" he demanded without bothering to identify himself to his sister when she answered her cell phone.

There was no need. Like everyone else in the department, Annabel would have recognized that growl anywhere.

"I'm at work, hunting for the Alphabet Killer like everyone else," Annabel told him. "Why?"

He winced at the gimmicky name she'd used. It was the kind of thing that caught on with the public like wildfire and fueled imaginations.

"Why aren't you with Zoe at her place?" Sam wanted to know.

"Because Zoe *isn't* at her place," Annabel pointed out. "She told me that she didn't want to miss work. When I couldn't talk her out of it, I figured she'd be all right in a public library. Did I figure wrong?" she asked hesitantly.

"No, but you should have called to tell me what you were doing," he said just before he terminated the call. The second he did, the phone began to vibrate insistently again.

Damn, but Annabel was fast, he thought.

Pressing the green accept bar on his phone without looking at the caller, Sam answered the call by saying, "It's okay, Annabel."

There was just the slightest hesitation on the other end of the call before a male voice asked, "Detective Colton? This is Dallas Jenkins of the *Houston Chronicle*. I've got some ques—"

The man never got any further with his inquiry.

Biting off a curse, Sam disconnected the call and then turned off his phone again. He knew he really should stay connected. Who knew what call he might miss by having his phone off? But twenty years ago, police detectives stopped at pay phones to make a call or used the transmitters in their squad cars to communicate. Doing without a cell phone was just his way of taking a trip down memory lane, he reasoned.

It was also his way of hanging on to his sanity, he silently added. Dealing with the press was liable to send him off in directions that wouldn't be advantageous to the investigation and right now, the investigation was of paramount importance—right after he got this one bit of business out of the way.

Driving down Main Street, he made his way to the town's public library. And found Zoe there, just as Annabel had said.

He stepped into the shadows to observe her for a minute, wanting to see what was so important that Zoe would risk her life to come back to it.

Zoe was helping a rather frazzled-looking student. It quickly became apparent the student was there to do research for a paper due the following morning—first period.

Standing off to the side and out of the way, hidden by the shelves, Sam eavesdropped as Zoe gave the teenager a few tips to help him with his research as well as a great deal of encouragement. Sam quickly gleaned the report was on Texas's battle for independence.

Waiting for Zoe to finish talking to the student, he began to actually listen to what she was saying. Listen with growing interest. That he did managed to really surprise him.

When the student finally went to finish working

with the information she had helped him gather, Sam came out of the shadows and into Zoe's line of vision.

"You actually made history sound interesting," he told her.

There was admiration in his voice, something that went a long way toward bolstering Zoe's own sagging self-esteem.

"History *is* interesting," she told him with a measure of enthusiasm.

If they could have gone on talking about history, she would have felt a great deal more at ease. But she knew he wasn't here about that. She could tell by his stance he wasn't here about something else, either. Something far more important than her ability to make an interesting subject even more interesting.

"You're not here to tell me you caught the killer, are you?" she asked, disappointed.

He wasn't going to insult her with any sort of promises about the future. Although he intended to pursue this killer to the ends of the earth, if he said anything like that, it would just sound like an empty vow. He was a man of action, not words.

"No," he told her. "I'm not. But how did you know that?"

Because I know everything about you. What makes you break down and smile, what makes you angry. What you won't talk about. Everything, she silently emphasized.

"You have a certain look on your face when everything comes together for you," she explained. "It's half triumphant and half peaceful, for lack of a better word."

It surprised him, but she was right.

Sam looked at her, puzzled. To the best of his knowledge, he hadn't been around Zoe all that much. They'd gone to the same schools—he knew because they were close to the same age and because *everyone* in Granite Gulch had attended the same set of schools—but he couldn't really recall being around her or even seeing her very much.

But there was no point in questioning Zoe about any of that now. He had more important things to concentrate on than that.

"I came to check on you," Sam told her. "I thought you'd be home."

She laughed quietly, as if the answer embarrassed her. "I can't hide at home forever. Besides, keeping busy is the best therapy. There're only two of us working the library floor and I can't have Alice doing all the work. That wouldn't be right," she concluded.

She was a great one for right and wrong, Sam couldn't help thinking. It was a shame some of her better traits hadn't rubbed off on Celia. He still wouldn't have asked her to marry him, but being forced to do so wouldn't have felt like such a hardship to him.

He was veering off the track, he reminded himself. He needed to get this over with. He owed it to Zoe. "I wanted to apologize to you."

Zoe's mouth dropped open. Recovering, she almost stuttered as she said, "Excuse me?"

"I owe you an apology," Sam told her. "I shouldn't have jumped all over you like that the other night. After all, I forced you to tell me what you and Celia were arguing about. It's not like you willingly volunteered the information."

She bit her lower lip, looking at him with concern shining in her eyes. Zoe wasn't savoring his apology. She was reliving his pain when he'd found out the truth.

"It wasn't right for Celia to lie to you like that. I told her she had to tell you the truth and she just laughed at me. That's when I stormed out. I was coming back to try to convince her one last time she couldn't build a marriage on a lie." The sigh that escaped her lips sounded more like a barely suppressed shudder. "But since she's dead, I should have left it alone and not mentioned the argument. There was no longer a need for you to know the truth."

She was being protective of him even after he had shouted at her. The woman was just an endless source of surprise to him.

He didn't think they made people like that. His mother had been like that, but his mother had been from another era. In his estimation, modern women were more concerned with being their own person and that came ahead of their concerns about others.

Men were the same way, Sam thought. He knew he was. It was a wonder the two genders ever got together anymore.

"I would have found out she lied anyway," he told

Zoe after a minute. He didn't want her to waste any more time beating herself up about it.

"How?" she asked him in surprise. "I don't think anyone else knew what she was doing. It would have put a damper on her marrying into the Colton family. Celia was smart enough to keep quiet about the deception. She only told me because she was confident I wouldn't tell anyone if she asked me not to. Family loyalty and all that," Zoe said in almost a dismissive tone. The latter caught Sam by surprise. "What Celia didn't count on was my being so horrified at the deception she was trying to pull off."

Sam was certain she would have undoubtedly kept the secret if he hadn't pressed her so hard to tell him. Zoe might have held truth to a high standard, but she was first and foremost loyal.

There was also one other little detail that both she and her sister had overlooked.

"There was something else Celia hadn't counted on," Sam told her.

Zoe frowned, thinking. She couldn't come up with anything. "What?"

"Being murdered," he told Zoe without any emotion in his voice. "By law, every murder victim has to have an autopsy performed on them."

Zoe's eyes widened as she looked at him. She knew what he was going to say next, but she was hoping against hope she was wrong. So she waited until he actually put it into words.

She didn't wait long.

"And Celia's autopsy gave us the cause of death—which was no mystery. It also made no mention of the fact that she was supposed to be three months pregnant—which *was* a mystery. Unless, of course, she'd never been pregnant to begin with," he concluded, looking pointedly at Zoe. "Which, apparently, she wasn't. You did tell me the truth back there, didn't you?"

Chapter 7

Zoe hadn't been really aware she'd been holding her breath until she felt herself letting it go and exhaling.

"Yes."

Since he'd read the autopsy report, Sam obviously had his proof and he knew now beyond a shadow of a doubt that, however much she'd resisted doing it, when he'd pressed her about it, she had told him the truth. What that meant was technically, she was off the hook because Sam knew she hadn't lied to him.

But where, exactly, *did* that put them?

Did he, despite his apology to her just now, hate her for having been the one who had made him aware of the harsh truth? Did finding out the woman he'd been noble enough to agree to marry had tricked him cause Sam to become even more bitter, more emotionally withdrawn than he already had been before Celia's deception had come to his attention?

Damn you, Celia, why did you have to mess with

Sam? Why couldn't you see what your lie would do to him? You ruined his life. He's never going to trust anyone ever again.

He's never going to trust me.

But the simple truth of it was her sister had always been self-centered. She had only been concerned about the way things would affect her, not how they affected anyone or anything else. She certainly never worried about her selfish actions having any kind of consequences.

And now Sam was going to suffer for her sister's thoughtlessness. And indirectly, because of the way it affected him and made him feel toward everyone in general, Celia's cheap trickery would affect her, as well.

Trying to come to grips with the present situation, she didn't realize Sam was asking her something until he was almost finished with the first sentence.

"Why did she do it?" Sam asked her suddenly out of the blue. "Why did she lie like that? Make me believe I had gotten her pregnant?" he questioned angrily. "She really had me going, made the room look like a hurricane had hit it that night she alleged I had sex with her."

He remembered how depressed he'd been that night when he came to see Celia. He'd never taken a life before, but that criminal had given him no choice. He found himself staring down the barrel of a gun and there was only a split second to make up his mind. A split second to choose to live—or to die.

He chose to live. And the criminal had died that night.

But it had still felt awful.

He'd had no one to talk to that night, so he had come to Celia because they had been seeing each other casually. And that night, he made an even bigger mistake. He drank too much. He'd done it to pass out so he could just get away from his thoughts, his guilt. But obviously he hadn't fallen asleep the way he'd thought.

Or so Celia had claimed.

And now, now he'd found out it had all been a lie and he'd passed out just the way he'd thought he had. The way he'd *wanted* to.

Did that make him a fool? Or just an easy target? Either way, he didn't feel good about it.

He should have known better and trusted his gut.

He looked so miserable, Zoe felt for him. Sam didn't lie and so he couldn't understand why anyone would lie. He especially couldn't seem to fathom why someone would go through the trouble of lying to him.

But Celia's reasons weren't all that hard to understand. "Because she knew you wouldn't marry her under normal circumstances, but if you thought she was carrying your baby, she was confident you'd step up and do the right thing. And she was right," Zoe concluded.

"Why would she want me to marry her?" he asked again. "Celia didn't love me." He realized that now.

Anyone who would resort to the kind of tricks and tactics Celia had didn't do something like that out of love, just out of some sort of selfish motive.

No, but I do, Zoe thought. Out loud, she told him what he wanted to know.

"Celia loved money and she loved looking down on people. Being married to a Colton would have allowed her to do both. In exchange," Zoe added on quickly, "she'd be a good wife."

Sam frowned. "You don't believe that," he said to her flatly.

"No," Zoe was forced to agree with a sigh. "But I could hope."

Sam laughed shortly as he told her, "Hope doesn't get you anything—except frustrated."

Oh, God, she wanted to take him into her arms, to comfort him the way someone would a child who'd had their heart broken, but she restrained herself. She knew he wouldn't react well to physical comfort like that. He just wouldn't allow it. Thanks to Celia, Zoe thought darkly, Sam had only gotten further entrenched into that isolated world of his.

Celia hadn't deserved to die the way she had, Zoe thought, but she hadn't deserved to have a man like Sam in her life, either.

"Well, that's all I want to say," he told her, bringing his reason for coming to the library to seek her out to an end. "I'd better get going."

She couldn't just let him leave this way. The thought

pulsed through her brain. Concerned, she acted before she could think to stop herself.

Catching hold of Sam's hand as he started to leave, she held on to it to keep him from walking out.

The look he gave her demanded an explanation. She really didn't have one to give him. Not one he'd understand at any rate.

"Are you going to be all right?" she finally asked, nearly tripping over the words.

He didn't answer her. Instead, he repeated what he'd already said to her a moment before. "I've got to get going." And then, in case that wasn't enough for her, he added, "I've got a serial killer to find."

He was right and she was standing in his way. He'd already taken time out of his day to come to apologize to her. She couldn't show her gratitude—or her understanding—by detaining him this way.

Zoe released his hand.

Sam walked out without looking back.

After he and the other people in the department had checked out all the calls that had come into the precinct regarding the so-called Alphabet Killer, Sam found himself no further along in the case than he already had been. Though he hated to admit it, he was still hovering around square one.

None of the calls had panned out, none of the so-called sightings had borne any fruit. Moreover, he and the department knew as much about the killer as they knew before, which was zero. There were precious few cameras throughout their small town—civilization hadn't quite caught up to the good people of Granite Gulch yet. Consequently, there was no video feed to pore over and no candid shots of the killer popping up in the places people swore they'd seen him.

Sam dragged his hand impatiently through his hair. He had no description whatsoever to work with. The only thing he had at all was a "type." They were hunting some obsessive-compulsive nutjob who killed women in their twenties who had long dark hair.

Not exactly a breakthrough or game changer.

"Why?" Sam asked, looking at the other faces who were gathered around him in the small living room of his brother Ethan's house. Because Ethan was the only one of them not in law enforcement, that somehow made his place neutral ground. Sam didn't know why that was important, but it felt right to him, so he'd asked the others to come here.

Because he trusted no one outside of himself and his siblings, he had turned to them for help rather than the people he worked with at the Granite Gulch PD. Currently, he was using his siblings as a sounding board.

Since it was part of their sworn duty, the law enforcement agents at the Granite Gulch police department were bound to search for this killer who was roaming about in their midst. But even so, they just didn't understand what was at stake here the way his brothers and sister did.

And, as they sat here now, Sam could almost read his siblings' minds.

That's what came of having gone through so many of the same things together, he thought. They'd all suffered the heartache of discovering their father had killed their mother. Because of that terrible incident, they were forcibly taken from their home and split up, exiled to different foster homes, where for the most part, misery and isolation was waiting for each of them.

They had also all experienced the shame of being known as the offspring of a deranged serial killer, a man who took his revenge on his older brother over and over again by killing strangers who looked like Big J. Big J's sin had been to buy him out of his share of a ranch.

Rootless and unlucky, Matthew failed at everything he tried his hand at—except for his killing sprees. He was painfully successful at that.

But even that finally came to an end. Caught, he'd been sent to jail. But his children continued to pay for his sins by going from foster home to foster home until they all aged out.

Only then did they finally come together, choosing to live in close proximity to one another in the town that had witnessed their shame, and, eventually, had watched them rally to win back their place in the sun.

What they had endured, together and separately,

made them closer to one another than they would ever be to another living human being.

And now, Sam hoped, maybe, just maybe, if they put their collective heads together, they could come up with a solution and find this killer whose behavior seemed to so closely mimic their father's MO.

"You know," Annabel ventured, "if the old man wasn't still in prison, I'd say this was his work."

"We're sure he's in prison, right?" Ethan asked, looking around at his brothers for confirmation.

Ethan's was a special burden because he had been the one who had come home early from school to find his mother dead by his father's hand. And he had been the one who had run all the way to a neighbor's house to tell them what had happened. Their mother's body was gone by the time the police got to the house—the old man had buried it somewhere—but it was because of Ethan that their father was eventually connected to the string of bizarre bull's-eye murders and sent to prison.

"Yes, we're sure," Trevor answered. He'd placed the call to the prison himself, as had, he felt it safe to guess, at least some of his brothers.

"You know," Ridge, who at twenty-nine was part of Search and Rescue during his work hours, spoke up, "they say this sort of thing can actually be in the blood." He glanced around the room, gauging his siblings' opinions. "They think it might be passed on from one generation to the next."

"So what are you saying?" Sam challenged. "That the killer is one of us?"

"No," Ridge quickly denied. None of them had seen Sam this edgy before. But then, these were extenuating circumstances, since the last victim had been Sam's fiancée. "But we're not all here," he pointed out. "One of us is missing."

"You mean Josie," Trevor said grimly.

"Yes." None of them had seen their youngest sibling in over six years, when at the age of seventeen, she had just dropped off the face of the earth, apparently by choice. "I hate to say it, but think about it," Ridge reluctantly pressed. "She's the only one who refused to have anything to do with the rest of us for no apparent reason. She even insisted the social worker tell us she never wanted any of us to get in contact with her. And then, a year before she ages out of the system, she just disappears." He paused and looked at the others. "Tell me that's not strange."

"I thought she ran off with that guy who asked her to marry her," Annabel said, bringing up the long ago incident.

Christopher, who had decided to make his living as a private investigator because he lived better by his own rules than having to obey the rules and regulations imposed by faceless superiors in some law enforcement agency, frowned as he recalled that time frame in Josie's life.

"You mean the one who dumped her and then was seen going around town with his new girlfriend?

Some girl with long dark hair and a killer figure?" he further recalled.

"Wait, say that again," Ridge requested, coming to attention on the sofa.

Christopher looked at his younger brother. At thirty-one, he was older than all of them, except for Trevor. "Killer figure?"

"No," Ridge said slowly, trying to reconcile the thought that was occurring to him with what he would prefer to believe. "You said a girl with long dark hair."

"Yeah, so?" And then Christopher's eyes widened as he realized what Christopher was leading up to. "Hey, you're not saying—?"

"I don't know what I'm saying," Ridge confessed. "But that description just seems a little too close to the description of the killer's last three victims to be a coincidence."

"You think it's Josie?" Trevor asked incredulously, joining in.

Ridge knew he didn't *want* it to be Josie, but he also knew they couldn't close their eyes to that being a possibility.

"I don't know what to think," he said honestly. "I'm saying it's one possibility."

"One far-out possibility," Sam retorted, clearly disagreeing with that speculation.

"Okay, there's one way to clear it all up," Ethan said to the others. "We need to find her so we can ask her what she's been doing with herself for the past six years since she dropped out of sight. Hell, who knows, maybe she's in some convent, atoning for the old man's sins."

But some of the others hadn't moved on from Ridge's suggestion.

"A female serial killer?" Christopher questioned. His dark eyes swept over his siblings. "We've been looking for a man."

"Maybe we need to rethink that, too," Ridge suggested.

"No, it's not Josie," Sam adamantly insisted. "She's been through a lot, but I refuse to believe she's turned into a serial killer."

"For what it's worth, I agree with Sam," Annabel told the others.

"I do, too."

The soft female voice had everyone turning around to see that Zoe had come out of the small room just off the living room and was now crossing the room to join them.

The first thing she was aware of was the way Sam was looking at her. He seemed both bewildered to see her there and somewhat annoyed she had invaded the space intended only for his family.

"What are you doing here?" he wanted to know, his voice far from friendly.

Now wasn't the time to fade into the shadows, although she really wanted to. She had to speak up for herself or she would never earn at least Sam's respect, if nothing more.

"I heard you were all getting together to pool your resources and see if you could come up with a way to track down the serial killer," she said, looking from one face to another. She quickly glossed over Sam's, afraid the recrimination she might see there would have her freezing. "I thought since the killer's last victim was my sister, I should be part of this discussion, too."

The answer didn't satisfy Sam. "How did you find out where we were going to be?" he demanded.

Zoe pressed her lips together, feeling it wasn't her place to tell him the name of the person who had given her that information. She didn't want to get anyone in trouble.

"I just did," she answered quietly.

That only seemed to annoy Sam more.

"I told her," Annabel said suddenly, speaking up. When Sam looked at her accusingly, she told him what Zoe had already stated. "I felt since Celia was the last victim, Zoe had a right to know where this investigation was going."

"She could find out the same way everyone else does, through the news broadcasts—or the internet," Sam snapped, deliberately ignoring the fact that Zoe was in the room. Seeing her was a painful reminder he couldn't trust anyone outside of his own siblings—and now he was beginning to wonder about that, as well.

"Let it go, Sam," Trevor told him. "Zoe's already here and maybe she's right. The last victim *was* her sister and also your fiancée. That unofficially makes her part of the family, as well, and as a member of the family, she has a right to be included in this."

Zoe flashed a grateful smile at Trevor as Sam bit off, "*Almost* part of the family."

"Don't quibble over words, Sam. It's beneath you," Ridge told him, joining in on the defense. "Zoe knew Josie back in the day. Maybe she has a helpful opinion on all this."

"I already gave it," Zoe reminded the Search and Rescue officer quietly. "I agree with Sam. Just because Josie was rejected by her boyfriend in favor of a woman in her twenties with long dark hair wouldn't automatically turn Josie into a serial killer. Besides, why now? Why would she wait all this time before going on this killing spree?

She looked around at Sam's brothers and sister. "You all knew your sister before any of this ever happened. Do you think she would be the type to turn into a cold-blooded killer?"

Ridge shook his head, frowning. "I wouldn't have said Josie was the type to sever all ties with her brothers and sister, either, but she did."

Zoe wasn't ready to accept the situation was so black and white. "Maybe there were extenuating circumstances that made her behave the way she did," she pointed out. It pleased her that she saw Sam grudgingly listening to her.

Zoe thought of Celia. Everyone had thought of her older sister as this wonderful, beautiful-looking girl, but Celia was deceitful and conniving and she had been from a very young age, using her looks to always get what she wanted. She thought nothing of manipulating people. And she bragged that she never felt a shred of remorse when things went her way.

"Not everything is always the way it looks," Zoe insisted.

"Zoe has a point," Trevor agreed, speaking up. "I don't think it's Josie, either, but we're not going to get to the bottom of that by sitting here and arguing about it. We need to find her," he said, agreeing with what Ridge had said a minute ago.

"You've got more resources for that than the rest of us," Sam pointed out.

"Which is why I'll put my team on it," Trevor answered.

"I'll give you the little I've managed to put together," Christopher told him. Trevor looked at him quizzically. "I've been looking for information on Josie's whereabouts ever since she disappeared." He looked around at the others. "I'll say one thing for our little sister. If she doesn't want to be found, she's done a damn good job of covering her tracks."

"That could also mean she's in the witness protection program," Ethan volunteered.

"Another possible avenue to explore," Trevor agreed.

"There's also another explanation," Ridge said, adding his voice to the discussion.

"You mean other than being in the witness protection program, or just not wanting to be found?" Christopher questioned.

"Yeah," Ridge answered grimly.

They all knew what Ridge was thinking and none of them wanted to say it out loud: Josie was in the same place as their mother.

"That's a last resort and for now, we're not going to talk about it," Sam told the others with a note of finality.

Nobody argued with him.

Chapter 8

"No."

The single word, firmly voiced, seemed to fill the entire room, seeping its way in through the walls of the house.

But Zoe didn't retreat. She stood her ground.

Sam was admittedly surprised the young woman didn't just absorb the force generated by his loudly voiced refusal and visibly shrink away from him. From his doorway, really, and back to the vehicle she'd driven over here. What little he remembered about Zoe—and although she had always been there, existing somewhere on the perimeter of his life, there wasn't all that much, but from what he did recall—she'd always been a timid, accommodating soul, easily manipulated.

This was neither timid nor accommodating, at least not in his point of view. She was being annoyingly stubborn.

"I'm coming along," Zoe informed him, ignoring his refusal.

She was well aware she didn't have a leg to stand on—especially not the two shaky ones that were holding her up right now. She had literally shown up on Sam's doorstep a few minutes ago and had stated her intentions when he had demanded to know what she was doing there. At that point, it seemed as if all hell had broken loose.

What had brought her to his doorstep was the same thing that had brought her to the roundtable meeting he had held with his siblings at Ethan's house to discuss their next move, both collectively and singularly. At the time she had been given a heads-up about the meeting by Annabel and although Sam had obviously not been happy about it, he'd grudgingly admitted that maybe she did have some right to be there. To find out what, if anything, they knew about the killer.

It had turned out they had no significant information regarding the killer's identity, but they did have a plan in order to hopefully, eventually, find out something.

To that end, Trevor was searching for Josie. But since the tips coming in from the public weren't leading to anything productive, Sam had decided to do what had only been mentioned previously in passing. Much as he would have rather done *anything* else, he had firmly made up his mind at that meeting to go talk to his father who was currently serving life without the chance of parole in the state prison fifty miles outside Granite Gulch.

He was pinning his hopes on the slim chance that his father was getting fan mail from some lunatic who was behind these serial killings. If that was the case, Sam felt certain the killer was undoubtedly writing to Matthew, bragging about being his disciple and the killing spree he was currently engaging in. With any luck at all, the killer would tip his hand and add in a description of one of the murders. If it matched what they already knew, then they had themselves a viable suspect rather than just a wistful wannabe.

Up until today, going to question Matthew at the sprawling, three-story state prison had been an option, but one he wanted to hold in reserve, leaving it as a last resort.

He no longer had that luxury.

Since there were no other options left open to him at the moment—and no new dead bodies to follow up on—this was the only course of action he could think of that might possibly yield him a lead.

But as much as he hated the idea of having to do it, he hated the idea of doing it with an entourage even more, even if that entourage consisted only of one person.

He was *not* about to let Zoe tag along. This wasn't some holiday fishing trip he was going on. This was immensely serious business.

"Don't you have a job to go to?" he all but shouted at her when Zoe refused to back off. "You know, books to alphabetize or whatever it is that librarians do these days."

"I don't know about librarians in general, but this librarian is taking a long, overdue vacation," she told him.

"So take it," Sam ordered angrily. "Go somewhere that people actually go when they take a vacation. Go to some theme park in mosquito country, or watch whales swim wherever it is they swim. Do something normal. *Nobody* goes to a prison on vacation," Sam informed her.

Zoe brought herself up to her full height and then rose a little farther on her toes, as if the extra inch could help her get her point across to him.

"I do," she countered.

When he turned his back on her to finish getting ready, Zoe didn't wait for him to slam the door, she pushed her way farther into his house. She had one chance to make her argument and she took it.

"This man ruined your childhood and nearly destroyed your family. He did destroy your mother and there are some people in the county who still hold things against your family because of the things Matthew Colton did." When he swung around to glare at her, Zoe refused to back down. Instead, she continued trying to make her point. "That's a lot of baggage to bring into a meeting."

"So, what, you're volunteering to be my baggage holder now?" Sam challenged, confused as to what point she was attempting to make.

Inside, she was cringing, but outwardly, Zoe forced herself not to flinch in the face of his erupting temper. Instead, she kept talking. "I thought having someone in your corner while you talk to your father might somehow make things a little easier for you."

Sam's face turned dark as his eyes narrowed, fixing their glare on her. "He's not my father. He's just someone who donated some DNA to my gene pool. It takes a lot more than that to be a father."

Zoe met his glare and didn't look away the way she instinctively knew he wanted her to.

"I agree."

"I don't care if you agree or not, you're not coming with me," Sam informed her firmly.

That should have been enough to get her to back down in his estimation—but it wasn't. The look in Zoe's eyes made him feel that he was losing ground. That wouldn't have happened with the Zoe he recalled knowing.

Maybe he hadn't really known her at all.

"I am—" she said with more conviction than she actually felt "—unless you have someone else who's coming with you."

"I do," he told her.

Surprised, she managed not to show it. Instead, Zoe challenged him on his assertion. "Who?"

He'd thought just telling her there was someone would be enough to make her back off and give up this ridiculous sidekick idea she had dreamed up. But obviously he'd thought wrong.

"You just don't give up, do you?" he retorted, stunned.

Her nerve was quickly dissolving. She wanted this to be over with—ending in her favor, and thus in his. Her eyes met his. Hers had defiance in them.

"Nope."

There was almost admiration in Sam's voice as he said, "I never knew that about you."

It wasn't in her not to be truthful. "Between you and me, neither did I," she confided. "But what it boils down to is I just can't let you go into that prison alone."

"I won't be alone," he told her. Then, when he saw she was waiting for more, he flippantly said, "The inmate count is at an all-time high at that prison they say."

Zoe managed to gather her flagging courage to her for a final rally. "This is where I'd laugh, because you made an attempt at a joke. But it's really not funny—and neither is your seeing that man alone."

This was getting tedious and he had to get going. The drive was long and boring and he wanted to get it out of the way and be done with it already.

"Get it through your thick head, Zoe, I don't need backup," he enunciated slowly and firmly, hoping to finally get through to her.

She ignored the insult and his patronizing tone. "I think you do. And if you don't let me come in with you, I'll still follow you there," she threatened, "and find a way to get in."

"So now you're breaking *into* prison?" Sam scoffed incredulously.

"Not exactly." God, but her mouth felt dry. "But I know people. I can get one of them to get me into the visiting area."

"What people?" he wanted to know.

It was obvious that he didn't believe her, but she refused to back down. "People-people," was all she ventured as an answer.

Sam laughed shortly as he shook his head in disbelief. He would have never thought this of her, never thought she could be this stubborn, this annoyingly unmovable.

There was obviously more to the woman than met the eye and maybe, if the stakes weren't so important—and he wasn't who he was—he might have been intrigued. But he *was* who he was and that meant he wasn't allowed to have a normal life. All he had was a job to do.

"You're bluffing," he told her, deliberately making his voice sound cold. It was his last attempt to scare her off.

He hadn't counted on just how stubborn she could be. "You don't know that for a fact—and *won't* know until you put me to the test."

Sam stared at her in disbelief. "You're just stubborn enough to get yourself into a hell of a lot of trouble, aren't you?"

"That's entirely up to you," she countered, surprising him further. "If you let me come with you, you'll be there to protect me," Zoe concluded simply.

Sam sighed. This was getting him nowhere and he had a feeling that short of leaving her tied up, Zoe was pigheaded enough to make good on her threat to follow him to the prison and maybe even into it.

"I can't begin to unscramble that and I don't have the time to even try." He was aware he was letting Zoe win by default, but he felt he had no choice. "Okay, you can come with me. But if having you there at the prison presents any sort of a problem at all, you're out, do you understand?"

"I understand," she answered solemnly.

It was a real struggle for her not to grin, but somehow, she managed.

They drove to the prison in silence.

Sam spent the entirety of the trip reviewing in his mind what he wanted to say to his father—while fervently wishing he never had to lay eyes on the man again. Had this not come up, had this new serial killer *not* had an MO so similar to the one Matthew Colton had employed more than two decades ago, he would have been completely satisfied to never see the man who was responsible for so much misery, both in his life and in general, ever again. Not even after he rotted away in prison.

But Sam was a law enforcement agent first, a wronged son second, so he had to put his own feelings aside in order to try to solve this crime that had all but fallen into his lap.

He was both relieved and at this point somewhat surprised Zoe said nothing during the drive to disturb the silence, leaving him to his thoughts and mental preparations. He had to admit, given her newfound backbone, he had expected her to talk at least part of the way to the prison.

But she kept quiet the entire time. So much so he slanted a glance in her direction several times before they finally saw the gray, forbidding gates of the prison looming in the distance.

"Having second thoughts?" he asked Zoe as they drove up to the prison and then waited for a guard to approach to open the gates and admit them into the inner perimeter within the compound.

Zoe saw two guards, armed with high-powered rifles, looking down at them from the observation tower high above the prison. She told herself it was for their own protection and tried not to be uncomfortable, but it wasn't easy.

"No," she answered, her firm tone masking the nerves underneath.

Sam studied her profile, saw the one twitch of her cheek. "I thought maybe that was why you've been so quiet."

Zoe brazened it out. "I figured you wanted to get your thoughts together. It's been a while since you saw him, hasn't it?"

Sam didn't have to pause to try to remember how

long it had been. He knew. Down to the minute. "Twenty years. I was five when the police came to take him away."

He remembered holding Josie's hand, telling her not to cry. He didn't know why he'd remained so stoic. Probably because he hadn't had any tears left to cry. He'd used them up, crying over his mother's murder.

She knew the story. But somehow, hearing Sam actually say it conjured up a vivid image in her mind of a little boy watching his father being dragged away, then helplessly witnessing his brothers and sisters being herded off in separate directions while he was being taken somewhere himself.

Tears shone in her eyes.

Out of the corner of his eye, Sam caught the glisten of tears in hers as he handed his identification to the guard who approached his window.

"You're not going to cry, are you?" he demanded.

"No," she answered quickly, tilting her head just a little.

She was trying to keep the tears from spilling out. She didn't want to have to wipe them from her cheek because that would give her away.

"Good. Because if you did, I'd have to leave you in the car," Sam told her harshly.

"I'm not crying," she told him firmly.

"So that's not a tear rolling down your cheek?" he asked, wondering just how far she was going to take this denial.

Despite all her efforts, one tear had managed to

cascade down, leaving a zigzag pattern in its wake. "No. That's an allergic reaction," she told him.

It made him laugh. Here he was in a situation he didn't want to be in, preparing to see and talk to a man he had never wanted to see again, and having it all witnessed by a woman who, by all rights, he should have been able to ditch hours ago sheerly through the power of his dark scowl.

There was nothing funny about any of it, and yet, she'd made him laugh by virtue of her ridiculously creative excuse.

"You've got guts, Zoe, I'll give you that," he told her. There was just a hint of admiration in his voice.

It made her smile.

She knew coming here with him was the right thing to do even if she hadn't felt about him the way she did. No one should have to go through something like what Sam was about to face alone and she wanted to offer him her silent support since no one else in his family had thought of it—or perhaps they had, but they knew he wouldn't allow them to come because he didn't want to appear weak in their eyes.

She was well aware Sam didn't care *what* she thought about him, because she didn't count. She was convinced the second she was out of his sight, she was also out of his mind.

The fact that he had come to apologize to her for the way he had acted when she had told him about Celia's deception had surprised her tremendously. But she felt that somehow the apology had probably been motivated by something that had to do with his job, not by something he felt personally because he *didn't* feel anything personally when it came to her.

Be that as it may, she still stood by her decision not to have Sam go through this alone and she would have stubbornly found some way to be there for him even if he had made things really difficult for her.

He meant that much to her.

"Last chance to back out," Sam told her as the guard waved them on. He looked at her for a long moment, waiting. He waited in vain. "This isn't going to be pretty."

"I didn't come to be entertained," she reminded Sam. "I came here for—because no one should have to go through something like this alone," she said, catching herself at the last minute.

She was repeating herself because she had almost said she had come here for him, and she knew that wouldn't have gone over well on any count. He didn't want her feeling he needed his hand held—and she knew he would have balked at the mere hint that her feelings for him had been her motivation.

Leaving her reason in the realm of generalization made it easier for him to accept her being there. Not easy—because God knew that nothing that had to do with Sam was ever easy—but definitely easier.

Having passed the guard, they drove slowly onto the compound. Driving quickly would have attracted attention—and distrust. So they crawled toward the parking area at a snail's pace.

Zoe used the time to look around and acquaint herself with the area. She'd never been there before, had no reason to have been there before.

It was all so depressing, she couldn't help thinking.

The prison had been built in an out-of-the-way area in Texas. So out of the way it would have been generous to describe it as desolate.

The feeling of loneliness and isolation seemed to throb from the very rocks and stones that had gone into the initial building's construction.

Escape from this prison had virtually never happened. Even if an escape *had* been successful, there was absolutely nothing to escape to.

There was nothing for miles and miles but more miles and miles. There was no cover, nowhere to hide. Any vehicle, coming or going, could be seen for miles in either direction. There were no woods to run to, no cover of any sort to hide behind or in. And in the summer, the sun made the exposure utterly intolerable.

In comparison, the prison itself was almost a welcome resort. It was, in essence, a very haven against the elements and a much less than benevolent Mother Nature.

The car, Zoe suddenly realized, had stopped moving. Lost in her observations, she hadn't noticed Sam had pulled into the visitors' parking area.

She'd only managed to unbuckle her seat belt when he came around to open her door.

"This is only going to work if you don't talk," he told her.

She nodded in response.

He took her silence as a sign of agreement. Sam's mouth curved ever so slightly in approval. He had no idea just how sexy that made him look to her. "Good."

Taking hold of her arm, he squared his shoulders and then ushered her with him as he walked up to the next guard.

It was time, Sam told himself, to meet the devil.

Chapter 9

Matthew Colton was already seated at the small, scarred table in the round communal room where inmates were allowed to meet with visitors on a limited, supervised basis during the prison's visiting hours.

This was not one of those occasions.

But exceptions had been made because Detective Sam Colton was a law enforcement agent and as such, was considered to be one of them. That entitled him, in certain unusual instances, extra courtesies. In this particular case, the exception had been made for privacy's sake. Aside from the prison guard, Matthew was the only other person in the room when Sam and Zoe entered.

As Sam approached the white-haired man, he exercised strict control not to show his initial surprise at what he saw. Matthew looked far older than his years. Not only that, but he looked ill, his face appearing grayer than his prisoner uniform. His once healthy pallor was now almost pasty, outward evidence of the fatal disease he was battling and had been battling, unsuccessfully, for a number of months now.

The prognosis, from what Sam had heard, was definitely not good.

The news of Matthew's cancer, when he had first heard it, had left him cold. As far as Sam was concerned, he'd been orphaned twenty years ago. The man he had come to see was merely an empty shell, the leftovers of a once evil, evil man who had regarded death as an equal partner in the life he had chosen to live.

Intense, probing, eerily blue eyes all but hidden beneath squinting lids studied him as he came forward. Except for their color, they reminded Sam of the eyes of a rattlesnake he'd once come across.

In his opinion, the rattlesnake had seemed friendlier—and more trustworthy.

"What's the matter, boy?" Matthew challenged bluntly, his voice scraping the air like gravel hitting against textured glass and cascading down. "Something wrong with what you sce?"

Sam sat down opposite his father, aware that Zoe had silently followed suit.

The Matthew Colton that had haunted his dreams as a child had been a large, hulking man. This man was nowhere near that man's size.

"Funny," Sam said when he finally spoke, "I remember you bigger."

The once broad shoulders, now slumped beneath

the weight of age and the cancer that was relentlessly eating away at him, rose and fell with an indifferent carelessness.

"Funny, I remember you smaller," Mathew retorted as he shrugged again. "We all live with our own perspectives." Eyes that now perpetually squinted at the commonplace world that was his reality took slow measure of the young woman sitting ramrod-straight beside his son. "What's this?" Matthew wanted to know. Then, before his son could answer, Matthew told him, "If you brought me a woman as a peace offering, you've wasted your money. I've got no use for them anymore."

Sam could feel his anger rising, settling in his chest like a fiery presence. It took effort to keep his voice level. "This is Zoe Robison, a friend," he said tersely. "And why in God's name would I be bringing you a peace offering?"

Matthew ignored the question as he looked even closer at the woman beside his son. "A friend, eh?" he scoffed in a manner meant to be belittling and ridiculing. "Men and women can't be friends. They can be lovers, or they can be enemies—usually when the female finds out he's been out tomcatting around on her—but they can't be friends." Matthew snorted. "You'd think a boy of mine would have more sense than that."

The choice of words instantly offended Sam. "I'm not 'your' boy." It was hard to keep the hatred out of his eyes. And even harder to keep it out of his voice, which seemed to resonate with it. "You gave up all claim to me and to my brothers and sisters the day you killed our mother."

Matthew's shallow face turned ugly. "If that's the way you think, then why the hell are you here?" the older man demanded.

This wasn't going well. She could see it in Sam's eyes, in his very body language. But he'd come this far. To blow up and just walk out now would lead them right back to the dead end they'd been repeatedly faced with, time and again. Matthew Colton might be their only way to find this new serial killer who had notoriously taken up Sam's father's mantle.

"Because we need your help," Zoe said, speaking up. She deliberately kept her face turned away from Sam, knowing he had to be glaring at her because she was doing exactly what he told her not to do. She was talking to Matthew.

"Oh, you do, do you?" Matthew asked, jeering at her. "And just why the hell should I help you?" he demanded, aiming his question at his son.

Damn, he hated this, Sam thought. He hated sitting here like some obediently transfixed little disciple, worshipping at the old man's feet. But he knew if he meant to solve these murders, he had no other choice.

"Because there's a serial killer on the loose and he's killing young women in their twenties with long dark hair," Sam began.

He was forced to stop talking while his father had a coughing fit that temporarily drowned out any words.

Finally, the coughing abated. Dragging a creased, dingy handkerchief out of his back pocket, Matthew Colton wiped his mouth and then his eyes, which had watered during the coughing spell.

Sucking in a ragged breath, the older man shoved his handkerchief back into his pocket. The look in his eyes, when he could finally focus them on his son, was malevolent.

"I've got cancer and maybe six months to live. Maybe less. Why the hell would I give a damn about some twenty-year-old tramps that are being offed?"

"They're not tramps," Sam informed him. "And you should give a damn because the killer's drawing red bull's-eyes with red dots on his victims' foreheads, just the way you did when you were killing men who looked like uncle Big J."

For a split second, there was a flash of interest in the opaque blue eyes. Interest—and something more. Sam could have sworn to it.

"You mean I got me a—what d'you call it?—a groupie?" Matthew asked with a harsh laugh.

"More like a follower," Zoe corrected the man quietly.

"A follower. Huh." Matthew turned the word over in his mind. Another coughing fit ensued, stealing more time away from him before he could ask, "So what do you want from me about this—this 'follower' that you claim I have?"

Sam tread lightly, knowing that any moment, his father could veer off in another direction, leaving him with his hat in his hand and nothing to show for it except for humiliation.

"You get a lot of mail in prison," Sam told him.

Matthew was immediately on the defensive, the way he had been for most of his life, no matter what the situation.

"So? There's no law against that," Matthew snapped defiantly, daring his son to say differently.

It was definitely a struggle for Sam to hold on to his temper when all he really wanted to do was hurl a few well-earned insults at his father and storm out.

Either that, or strangle the man with his own bare hands.

Neither could get him what he wanted and this, he told himself, wasn't about him. It was about the serial killer's victims. The victims and their families who were left to come to terms with dreadful losses that would wound anyone's soul.

"No, it's not," Sam agreed. "But did any of these letters—especially ones you might have received in the past few months," Sam qualified, "stand out as a possible copycat in the making to you?"

Matthew cocked his head and looked at him myopically. "Copycat?"

"You know, someone obsessed with you and your MO," Sam explained further, hating every word he was forced to relay. "Maybe asking you for a lot more details about the cases that the press might have left out."

Matthew seemed to take umbrage at having the

term clarified. "I know what *copycat* means, boy. I'm not dumb."

"Nobody said you were," Sam replied, schooling himself to hold on to his temper and not snap at the man sitting opposite him.

As he spoke, he studied his father.

The old man was stalling, Sam thought. There was something in Matthew's body language, in the look on his sunken face, that made him think that. There was only one reason for it. His father was stalling because he knew something and he was trying to decide how best to make it pay off.

Everything, Sam knew, had always been about him for his father. No one was even a close second.

"You know something, don't you, old man?" Sam said. As he said the words, it felt as if his entire body had gone on alert and come to attention.

Matthew sneered. Having the upper hand had always been all-important to him.

"I didn't say that."

"You didn't have to," Sam told him. "I can see it in your eyes."

Anger rattled in Matthew's voice. "There's nothing in my eyes except for disappointment. Disappointment that none of you 'fine, upstanding young citizens' ever came by for so much as a visit. And now you want my help. Well give me one good reason why I should help you," Matthew challenged malevolently, his whole countenance turning ugly.

"Because it's the decent thing to do," Sam snapped angrily.

"Not interested," Matthew retorted. "I don't give a damn about decent." And then a devious, conniving look entered the man's watery eyes. "Tell you what I do give a damn about. I give a damn about getting some extra TV time—and a special massage pillow to help soothe this aching body of mine. Oh, yeah, and some pecan pie. For starters," he added significantly.

Sam stared at him in complete disbelief. "You want pecan pie."

"For starters," Matthew stressed, taking on a superior tone.

Sam couldn't help himself. His temper surged until it was all but out of control.

"You smug, arrogant SOB, you think this puts you in the driver's seat, don't you? That it lets you dictate terms just because you may or may not have some information to dangle in front of us? Well, I don't believe you." Sam's complexion reddened as he struggled not to shout his outrage over the game he felt his father was playing. "I don't believe you have any real information to offer in exchange, because all you've ever done is lie, cheat and kill your whole miserable excuse of a life."

As he spoke, Sam's fury just seemed to grow to dangerous excesses.

But he wasn't finished yet.

He hadn't gotten to what bothered him most.

"Trevor and I have been waiting for years for you

to tell someone where you buried our mother so we could give her a proper burial and maybe, just maybe finally put that awful chapter of our lives to rest. But you never said so much as a single word. So why should I believe you've suddenly changed and you're willing to tell me what I need to know for a pillow and a damn pie?" he wanted to know, his face all but contorted in anger.

"Pecan pie," Matthew interjected, almost taunting him.

Sam had had enough. This was going nowhere and he refused to allow his father to manipulate him any further for his own amusement.

"Let's go, Zoe," Sam ordered, getting to his feet. There were daggers in his eyes as he looked contemptuously at the old man. He'd wasted enough time here. "He doesn't know anything."

Turning away from his father with finality, Sam began to walk away and he had absolutely no intentions of ever coming back.

He and Zoe were nearly at the door, about to signal to the guard to open it and let them out, when he heard Matthew call out.

"There's something much bigger I want in exchange for telling you kids where your mama's buried."

Sam wanted to keep going. To walk out the door and never look back. But he knew if he did that, he would be permanently turning his back on the possibility of *ever* finding where his mother was buried.

And even a slim possibility was better than no possibility at all.

It was for her, not for himself, not even for the victims, that he decided to turn around again.

But even as he wrestled with his conscience, he felt Zoe lace her fingers through his. She gently tugged on his hand, silently urging him to turn around and give the old man the audience he craved.

He knew she was right even as he resisted. And in the end, he glared at the man, but he went back to playing the game.

"What?" Sam asked. "What is it you want in exchange for giving us that information?"

Matthew didn't answer right away. He couldn't. Another coughing fit had seized him and this one lasted longer than the other two. Long enough to alarm Sam despite the fact that he didn't show it.

He was surprised when Zoe took out her own handkerchief from the small shoulder bag she had and then used it to wipe the beads of sweat that had popped out on his father's brow.

Managing to regain his composure, Matthew nodded his thanks in her direction.

He struggled to get air into his lungs at a steady rate before he attempted to answer the last question his son had put to him.

"It's something I want to be buried with," Matthew told him.

Sam hadn't a clue what the old man was going on

about, or what he could have possibly wanted next to him when he was finally put into the ground.

He had stopped thinking in terms of having a funeral for his father a long time ago. For his money, Matthew Colton's remains could be scattered in a potter's field, to stay there for all eternity.

Either that, or just be cremated, his ashes thrown into some ravine.

That the old man was thinking in terms of an actual burial—and with some kind of item no less—was a complete and total surprise to him.

"What?" Sam asked impatiently, thinking his father was deliberately dramatizing the moment.

Was there a box stored somewhere? A box filled with the trophies he'd taken from his victims to remind him of all his kills so he could relive them? Was that what the old man wanted to be buried with?

He wouldn't have put it past Matthew.

Opaque blue slits met and held his eyes. "It's an old watch."

This made even less sense. "What old watch?" Sam demanded.

Granted he hadn't seen his father since he was five, but up until that point, he couldn't recall there being some sort of special watch that his father wore or was never without.

This had to be a bunch of bull, Sam thought. But if so, to what end? To string him along?

Or—?

"I hid it on a property clear across Texas," Matthew told him. "I need someone to get it for me." He pinned Sam with his intense gaze. "Somebody I know won't make off with it."

"So suddenly I'm trustworthy." Sarcasm dripped from Sam's lips. "Interesting."

"You're a police detective. An *honest* police detective, which is almost as rare as a damn unicorn and not nearly as pretty," Matthew said with contempt. "I don't know how the hell that happened, given that you're my son, but you are, and I might as well make some kind of use of it," he said flippantly. His eyes narrowed until they very nearly disappeared altogether. "So, we got a deal?" he wanted to know.

Considering the fact that Matthew was the one who was setting down terms and asking for things without first volunteering a damn thing of his own, Sam knew he'd be a fool to say yes outright. And the one thing he did remember about his father was that the man had no use, and even less respect, for fools.

"I've got to talk it over with the others. I'll get back to you on that," Sam replied.

"Oh, you do, do you?" Matthew sneered. "Well, while you're doing all this conferring with those other losers, here's something more to talk to them about," his father added, seemingly out of the blue. "I want to see one of you—a different one—on the fourth Friday of every month."

"And if they don't want to come?" Sam challenged.

"Oh, they'll come all right. If they want to find out where their mama's buried, they'll come," Matthew said smugly. "The way it'll work is after each 'loving' visit, I'll give each of them a clue. You kids put all the clues together—and you're really, really smart—you'll get your answer where I buried her," Matthew concluded.

"You're playing games?" Sam asked, outraged.

In response, Matthew shrugged. "I've got nothing else to do. And, as an added bonus for you, just 'cause I'm feeling generous, I'll let you have those letters you were asking about. Letters from my admirers," Matthew laughed harshly. "I'll even throw in a couple from people who hate my guts, just to add a little variety to the pot."

Sam didn't trust himself to say anything. Instead, he turned away and this time reached the door. "I'll get back to you," he said again, not even bothering to turn around.

"Don't take too long," Matthew called after him.

The senior Colton remained sitting at the table they had just shared. He didn't trust his legs to support him and he refused to show any signs of physical weakness around his son. Despite his age and his condition, he refused to relinquish his image. Image was everything in his narcissistic world.

"Hey, another girl could meet her end while you're thinking things over," he called after his son. "Wouldn't want that on your conscience now, would you, boy?"

Even in this dire situation, with perhaps six months to live, perhaps less, apparently Matthew could still find enjoyment in taunting him, in using the extreme distress of others to bolster his own situation and sense of importance.

"A lot you care," Sam shot back.

The laugh was nasty, cold, and so like his father. "You're right. I don't."

A fresh rage swept over Sam. For two cents—less—he'd just keep walking and never come back. But as he had told himself before, this wasn't about him. It was about his poor mother, who after all these years still didn't have a place of eternal rest.

And it was about some nameless, faceless young woman who had her whole life in front of her and had absolutely no idea that life might come to a jarring, extremely painful end within a matter of days—if not hours.

Sam was hell-bent on stopping the murderer and as much as it killed him, he needed his father to do it.

And that meant he had to come back. Come back and play the game Matthew Colton required of him. If he didn't, he and his siblings would never know where their mother's remains currently were, and equally as bad, there was the strong possibility that several more young women would meet their untimely end.

Squaring his shoulders, Sam kept walking, cursing his father, and the fate that had bonded them in this macabre fashion, in his heart.

Chapter 10

In deference to Sam's private nature, Zoe refrained from saying anything when they left the prison.

As they made their way back to his car, she could feel Sam seething and struggling to come to terms with what had gone down during his conversation with his father in the prison's visitation room. Even so, she refrained from saying anything until they were seated inside his vehicle.

But she really hated seeing him having to go through this.

Just how much more could he be expected to take? Zoe wondered, her protective instincts rising to the surface. His mother had been taken from him at a young age, his father had literally torn his family apart, the woman he thought was carrying his child had deliberately deceived him for her own gain and now his father was attempting to play him, dangling much-wanted information in front of his face as if it was some sort of a carrot. To what end, no one could really guess.

Certainly not her, Zoe thought, waiting for Sam to get into the car on his side.

Pulling her seat belt out and around her waist, she then reached over to slip the metal tongue into its slot and looked at the man she had silently loved since forever.

Zoe broke her silence.

"Sam, you can't let him get to you."

Sam's eyes narrowed as he glared in her direction. He jabbed his key into the ignition. "Did I ask you for your opinion?" he demanded hotly, still smarting from the fact that he had no choice in this matter with his father. He was going to have to go along with Matthew's manipulative game.

He *hated* not having a choice.

"No," she replied quietly. Zoe shifted in her seat and faced forward, looking, without seeing, through the windshield.

Ashamed of the way he'd just jumped all over her when all she had done was try to be there for him—never mind that he hadn't asked her to—Sam felt a sharp jab of guilt rip right through him.

"Sorry," Sam mumbled his apology, and then immediately went on the defensive. "But what makes you think he got to me?"

In his somewhat biased opinion, he had done his best to sound indifferent to his father's ramblings, and when that didn't have the desired effect, he'd just stepped back and let the old man talk without bothering to answer him. How was that letting Matthew get to him? At least visibly?

"Well, for one thing, I seem to have lost all feeling in my fingers," Zoe informed him quietly, looking down at her hand, which was now captured in a vise lock in his.

Somehow, without thinking, he'd taken hold of her hand again. Not only that, but he obviously must have squeezed it, channeling his feeling through the grip he'd exhibited, holding her fingers virtual prisoners in his hand. No wonder she thought something was wrong.

Instantly he released Zoe's hand and then looked at it. He saw what she was talking about. The fingers on that hand all looked rather red and he could see they were all but pulsating.

"I did that?"

She smiled at the wonder in his voice. "Well, they weren't like that before," she said without putting the blame on his doorstep.

He sighed. He'd let Matthew get to him and that in itself really annoyed him. "Sorry."

Zoe merely nodded, indicating her tacit forgiveness. "I understand."

Now that was just a lot of bull, he thought irritably. She could be sympathetic, but there was no way she could even remotely understand what he'd been through and what he *was* going through.

"No, I don't think that you do," he contradicted,

his voice low, dangerous, even as he tried to temper it. "You had a normal childhood. You weren't made to feel like some kind of a freak, an outcast, because *your* father killed *your* mother." He thought of Josie. "You didn't hear your little sister shrieking in fear as she was being dragged off, away from the only family she'd ever known—the way we were *all* dragged away from each other eventually."

Sam was right, Zoe thought. She hadn't gone through any of that. But it didn't lessen her feelings of empathy even by an iota.

But she didn't want to argue the point. That would only aggravate him and her goal was to calm the man down, not get him even more worked up than he already was at this point.

"I just meant I can understand your being angry and hurt even if I didn't have the same things happen to me," she explained patiently.

Her manner—and her obvious forgiveness of his brusque manner—just made him feel guilty again. But she *knew* he was like this. Why did she continue trying to push this conversation with him, as if it was something they could eventually come to some sort of an agreement about? Why didn't she just give up and go?

"Why are you sticking around, Zoe?" he asked her out loud. "I keep jumping down your throat. Why are you sticking around?" he repeated.

"Because you need somebody," she answered simply. "You're angry and in your present state, you're not likely to make many friends, so I thought I'd be that friend for now."

"I don't need any friends," he informed her. And then his tone softened. He'd been convinced they didn't make people like that anymore, and yet here she was.

Finally starting the car and then peeling out of the space, he glanced at her for a moment before looking back at the road. "You know you should run for the hills, don't you?"

He caught her grin in the rearview mirror when he glanced up. There was something almost stirringly appealing about it.

"Sorry," she told him, "I never was very bright."

Sam had no idea what possessed him. Why he suddenly veered to the side of the road, threw the transmission into Park and pulled up the handbrake even though the vehicle continued to idle impatiently, shuddering and all but bucking as it expressed its need to get back on the road.

But he did.

And when he did, and Zoe looked at him with a silent, uncertain question in her eyes, he took her face between his hands and without a single word to precede his action or to warn her of what was coming, he pressed his lips against hers.

Hard.

Maybe it was his need for some sort of human contact after having maintained that barbed wire fencing around his emotions for so long. Maybe it was because in a world of self-serving people, Zoe was the only truly genuine person he had come across in so many years, he couldn't remember the last time that he had, and that made her rare.

Or maybe, just maybe, it was the only way he felt he had to scare her away and make her run from him while she still could.

Whatever the reason that motivated him to do what he did, he discovered an entirely different reaction waiting to ensnare him on the other side of that one lone, unplanned action.

The incredible sweetness of Zoe's mouth pulled him in, made him step outside himself, outside his anger, and just experience the closest thing to purity he had ever encountered.

He had kissed her so abruptly, in part, to shake her up and he had wound up being the one who was shaken. Hastily ending the kiss as suddenly as it had been initiated, he pulled back, stunned and momentarily speechless as he stared at her.

What the hell had he just gone and done—besides complicate things exponentially and open himself up to a whole host of things he neither wanted nor knew how to deal with?

What the hell was I thinking? that same voice demanded in his head.

That was just the problem. Maybe for that small increment of time, he had stopped thinking altogether and had just gone with pure, instinctive reactions.

"I'm taking you home," he growled, gunning the car's engine.

She knew he didn't believe in talking and she wasn't about to press him for some long discussion about what had just happened. But she wasn't about to just be tossed aside like some inconsequential gum wrapper, either.

"Sam—"

"Not another word," he warned, his voice low, raspy as he struggled to get himself under control. "Not another damn word, or I can't be held responsible for what happens next."

"You'd never hurt me," Zoe told him, her own voice soft, like spring raindrops against a window pane.

She seemed a lot more confident of that than he was. "Don't be so damn sure," Sam bit off.

"But I am."

There was no hesitation in her voice, no coyness either. She wasn't like anyone he had ever known and that confused the hell out of him.

Sam's hands tightened so hard on the wheel, he came close to losing control of the vehicle. Right now, this moment, he wanted nothing more than to just lose himself in this woman who seemed to be everything good that was no longer in his life.

But he knew it would be a mistake—for him *and* especially for her.

So he kept driving, staring straight ahead at the road and forcing himself to think of nothing more than getting the next clue, finding the next piece of the puzzle.

And most of all, what to say to convince his siblings to play Matthew's game.

As if reading his mind despite the blanket of silence that had descended on her side of the vehicle, Zoe said, "I can help you convince them."

Caught off guard and surprised by what she was telling him, he spared Zoe a quick glance—anything more might just have him careening off the road again and he wasn't the type to make the same mistake twice.

"Them? Who are you talking about?" he asked almost belligerently, thinking his manner would frighten her away from the subject and make her forget about any half-baked offer she was making.

But he was beginning to see that once her course was set, this new, different Zoe wasn't about to be derailed, at least not easily.

"Your brothers and Annabel. I could help you convince them to go along with your father's so-called 'rules of the game.'"

Even the term sounded full of itself—that was Matthew Colton all the way, Sam thought angrily. Completely full of himself.

He turned on Zoe and challenged, "And just why the hell would you be any better at convincing them than I would?"

"You're family," she pointed out without any bravado. "Sometimes, it's easier to say no to family, but if someone outside that close-knit circle asks for a favor, then it's considered and most likely, it gets granted. As almost all law enforcement agents, your siblings are public servants and as such, they're obligated to listen to the public.

"I can also make it personal," she went on. "You're hunting my sister's killer and I both need and want answers. There's only one way that could possibly happen. If they go along and play Matthew's game, I could very well get those answers."

He was clearly impressed by her persuasive reasoning. This was a side of her he had never even suspected existed.

"Is that what you learn, being a librarian?" he asked, thinking of all those reference books she was surrounded with.

"No, that's what I learned, being a person," Zoe corrected.

Determined, only a few minutes ago, to cut her loose and keep her away from anything that had to do with this mess that was his life, Sam began to waver about his position.

To give Zoe her due, he supposed she was making sense. And, when he came right down to it, it wasn't as if he couldn't use the assistance. He knew how everyone else felt about dealing with the old man—just slightly more open to it than to dealing with the plague.

When he came to a stop at a red light, Sam gave the

woman he was beginning to realize he really didn't know at all a long, hard look.

"You know, I used to think of you as a pushover, that you were easily swayed by everyone else's opinions. I'm beginning to think maybe I should really reassess that image."

"Maybe you should," she agreed with more than a hint of a triumphant—not to mention secretly relieved—smile curving her generous mouth.

"But for now, until I can get everyone together again," Sam went on, "I'm still going to drop you off at your home."

Zoe nodded. She actually wanted to remain with him, to help him in the investigation in any possible way she could, but she knew she couldn't protest every little thing he proposed that she was less than thrilled with.

Zoe knew the value of picking her battles and this one was just going to have to fall by the wayside—at least for now.

To his surprise, Sam managed to get all his brothers and his sister together in order to report the outcome of his prison visit and he did it within just a couple of hours.

Then, though he was having second thoughts about it, he remained true to his word and allowed Zoe to join them. But only on the condition that she kept quiet unless it looked as if he really needed—*and wanted*—her help in convincing his siblings to go along with Matthew's rather bizarre demands.

In effect, Zoe was his plan B.

Just before he got started, Sam told the others she would be sitting in on this. Everyone was polite and greeted her accordingly, obviously waiting for either Sam or her to explain things further.

But Zoe said nothing—as she had already agreed—and Sam launched into his narrative, giving every indication he was less than pleased about the way things had turned out.

Everyone quickly forgot Zoe was there, as hurt, angry feelings flared around the room.

Ethan was the first to put it into words.

"I don't like it," he protested heatedly. "This makes that old SOB feel as if he's the one holding all the cards." Bitterness twisted his mouth as he thought of the past, of coming home and seeing his mother lying there, dead, while Matthew hovered over her, painting that sick bull's eye on her forehead. "All these years, we've been asking him where Mother's buried and he ignored us, acting like we were all less than nothing—just sand fleas biting at his ankles. And now, all of a sudden he gets handed a medical death sentence, so he wants to play, because he gets to say 'Jump' and we get to say, 'How high?'"

Ethan shook his head, all but shutting down right in front of the others. "No, count me out. I'm not doing this. I'm not going to feed that monster's ego. Tell him to find someone else to torture."

Zoe looked around the room, seeing the same sentiment written on the faces of Sam's other siblings. Glancing in his direction, she saw no indication Sam wanted her to say anything.

But this wasn't going to go well from here and she couldn't just sit by and say nothing. Not when this was so important.

"Maybe it's not his ego you're feeding," she finally interjected, her quiet voice a marked contrast to the Colton crew's steadily rising voices.

Sam's head jerked in her direction. "Not now, Zoe," he warned, thinking she was only going to succeed in getting everyone angrier.

But Zoe stubbornly persisted. "Maybe it's Matthew's need to reconnect before he dies that's motivating him to make this strange arrangement."

"What are you talking about?" Ethan demanded while the others looked in her direction, curious to hear what she had to say next.

Sam's protective instincts spiked, but he refrained from saying anything, wanting to see what Zoe would say in response.

She felt as if she had treaded on shaky ground, but she was determined to get her thoughts across. It was important to Sam and to the others that they see the matter the way she did. She had the right amount of distance from the situation to be able to see more than they did. For one thing, she had never been wounded by the senior Colton the way they had.

"Matthew's dying and he knows he only has a

few months to live. He also knows his family wants nothing to do with him, but now, in the last days of his life, he realizes that maybe he's more like other people than he'd want to admit—he wants to see his family, to have someone mourn his passing.

"Being Matthew, he's not going to beg you to come see him—but he can *make* you come to see him in order to secure these pieces of the puzzle he's holding just out of reach. It's all he has," she concluded, painting the older man for the sad, sorry excuse of a human being he was.

"He just likes being in control and manipulating us," Ridge said bitterly.

"Maybe, but he also wants to *see* you," Zoe pointed out. "If he didn't, he'd have different requirements before he gave up the information. Think about it," Zoe implored, looking around at Sam's siblings.

For a few moments, there was silence. Silence that seemed to drag on.

And then Annabel broke it by saying, "I think she's right."

"Yeah," Sam agreed, glancing at Zoe. "I hate to admit it, but—yeah, I think so, too."

Ethan sighed. It was obvious he wanted to hold out. But just as obvious that he knew he couldn't.

"Okay," he said, looking at Zoe instead of Sam, "count me in."

After that, the rest just fell into place, with each of them taking a month, at the end of which time they would hopefully have all the pieces to the puzzle that would finally lead them to the spot where their mother was buried.

It was a goal they all held in common.

Chapter 11

By now, Sam had come to the realization that he couldn't talk Zoe out of doing what she felt she needed to do, so he didn't waste his time or his breath in even trying. Which was why Zoe returned to the prison with him the following day.

As before, Matthew Colton was already seated at the table in the communal visiting area, waiting for him when he entered the room with Zoe. It occurred to Sam that as of yet, he hadn't seen his father walk in on his own power and he began to wonder why. Both times the senior Colton was already seated and Sam suspected there might actually be a reason behind the orchestrated scene. Most likely, his father, despite battling the ravages of cancer, didn't want to exhibit any sort of physical weakness in front of his offspring. And that, he was certain, strictly had to do with image, not any sort of parental feelings on Matthew's part.

The cold-blooded killer had never cared about any of them.

What Zoe maintained yesterday notwithstanding, he felt Matthew was incapable of any sort of feelings for anyone—other than himself.

So, Sam concluded, to Matthew it was important to maintain a facade, an image of strength no matter what. Which, ultimately, was the lethal disease systematically destroying his insides.

The squinting eyes grew even more so as Matthew watched them approach him.

"Well, well, well, if it isn't Romeo and Juliet, back again."

The smug, sneering look on the pale, sunken face looked particularly evil to Sam. For a split second, he came very close to turning on his heel and taking Zoe with him.

"This is getting to be a regular habit now, isn't it?" Matthew asked, laughing.

The laugh was interrupted by a coughing fit that succeeded in temporarily angering the senior Colton. When he could finally catch his breath again, Matthew gestured to the other two seats at the table.

"Well, sit down. Talk. You are here to talk, right?" he pressed, pinning his youngest son down with a penetrating look that dared him to pretend otherwise.

"You've got what you want, old man," Sam said grudgingly.

For once, Matthew didn't endeavor to draw the scene out, didn't attempt to be coy. Instead, he went directly to the heart of the subject, watching his son's face closely. "They'll come?"

"They'll come," Sam verified. "One each month, just the way you specified. Now all you have to do is live up to your part—and stay alive," Sam added, almost daring him to keep his word.

Matthew dissolved into another coughing fit before he could answer. When he finally stopped, there was moisture in the inner corners of his eyes, not from any spent emotion, but from the toll that trying to refrain from coughing took on him. For several moments, there was only the sound of the older man's heavy breathing.

"I'll do what I can." After a dramatic pause, Matthew tapped his palm on the top of the rectangular white box that was sitting in front of him on the table. It looked like the kind of box a heavy winter coat might be put in just before it was wrapped up and given as a gift. "I'm a man of my word," he told Sam.

Sam had to bite his tongue to keep from saying what he wanted to regarding his father's so-called "word" and the honor that implied. Instead, he reached for the box.

Matthew looked almost reluctant to raise his hands and release his claim to what was inside.

Sam assumed the box contained the letters he had asked for.

In part, Sam guessed, the letters stroked the old man's ego, kept his spirit going. He knew Matthew basked in the gory reputation he had earned. At this point, Sam supposed it was all the old man had, which made the convicted serial killer just that much more pathetic in his eyes.

And what is it that you have? Sam asked himself. *How full is your life? When you die, who's going to remember you?*

This was stupid. He didn't have time for self-examination, Sam upbraided himself. And this was definitely *not* the time to let Matthew get to him.

Matthew slowly raised his hand away from the box, indicating by his action that he was giving his son permission to take possession of it, and perforce, the letters that were inside.

"Those are they," Matthew said needlessly, his voice particularly raspy. "All the letters I got in the past six months." He raised his chin, something, Sam noted, that seemed increasingly more difficult for the old man to do, and stated rather proudly, "I didn't hold nothin' back. That's all of them. The good, the bad and the ugly."

The last statement was followed by a deep laugh which then, in turn, was followed by his hacking cough. It was beginning to seem that one could not come without the other.

"There's over a hundred of them," Matthew told them. "And when you're done readin' them, I want them back, you hear? I'm only lendin' them to *you*, nobody else. I don't want nobody else snooping in my life," Matthew dictated imperiously.

"A little late for that, isn't it?" Sam asked sarcastically.

A response to which Matthew smiled a smile that, to Zoe's way of thinking, brought a new definition to the word *evil*. She had to actually steel herself off to keep from shivering from the chill that shimmied up and down her spine.

"You don't know everything, boy," Matthew informed him with perverse pride. "Nobody does."

Sam's face darkened. "And what's that supposed to mean?"

At that moment, Matthew seemed to come alive right before their eyes, his own eyes widening just enough to display blue eyes that were almost sparkling.

"Just what I said." And then his eyelids drooped again, as if the effort to keep them open was far too much for him. Matthew nodded at the box. "And don't think about holding any of those back. I know exactly what's in there."

Sam had had just about as much as he could stomach for one morning. He rose again to his feet. Zoe was quick to follow suit.

"Right," Sam responded. "I'll get back to you, old man," he said as he turned away, taking the box and tucking it under his arm as if it was a rectangular football.

It felt heavy, he thought, really heavy. He was tempted to open it to make sure there was nothing in the box except paper, but he had an uneasy feeling that was something Matthew was counting on. He could be wrong, of course, and it was just his imagination, but he was taking no chances. He'd done enough to sate the man's ego for one day.

Matthew raised his voice. "Yes, you will."

The words followed Sam out of the room as the guard unlocked the door, letting him and Zoe leave the room and Matthew's presence.

He had to police himself not to release a loud sigh of relief.

Only after he had regained control over himself did Sam look toward the woman who had insisted on silently being there for him. He wondered if her presence had a calming effect on him, or if it had all been just a coincidence.

"Had enough?" Sam asked her.

Rather than answer yes or no, Zoe replied, "I'm okay." Looking at the box he had tucked under his arm, she couldn't help asking him, "Are you taking that home with you?"

"This filth?" Despite the weight, he had to look to reassure himself that the box he'd tucked under his arm was still there, that it hadn't just disappeared somehow, like a cheap magic show trick. He wasn't putting *anything* past his father. "No, I don't want it in my house. It's bad enough I've had to live with so much of what was going on in my head. No, this is going down to the station."

She looked surprised that he was taking it to work.

"I thought you told your father you weren't sharing this with anyone."

Sam stopped in front of his vehicle and aimed his key fob at it. He lost no time in opening the driver's side door, depositing the seemingly ordinary looking box in the back seat.

"No, that was what *he* said. If you recall, I didn't say anything. I didn't agree to his terms or tell him where he could go and stuff them." Sam got in behind the wheel and closed the door. "It's easier to let him think what he wants to think."

Zoe quickly got in on her side. Sam had aroused her curiosity. "But if he would have pressed you, would you have lied?"

Sam stopped what he was doing and looked at her, surprised. "The apple doesn't fall far from the tree, is that what you're thinking?"

Zoe secured her seat belt then shifted in her seat so she could face him as she told him, "No, that never crossed my mind. I just wanted to know if you're too principled to lie."

He laughed dryly. "Is that what you call it? 'Too principled'?"

She shrugged, not sure if he was making fun of her, or if he was just trying to get an answer out of her. "It's as good a term as any."

His key still in his hand, for the moment Sam left it out of the ignition as he decided to turn the tables on her. "How would you feel about something like that? About lying to get to the truth faster?"

In all honesty, he expected Zoe to be indignant at the idea of being accused of even considering telling a lie. He fully expected her to support a road that was straight and narrow because that was what she made him think of: the straight and narrow.

"I'd do whatever it took to save someone from being senselessly killed," she told him simply. Then, just like that, she changed topics. "Two people reading the letters would cover twice as much ground as one person."

"Two," he repeated, furrowing his brow as he slanted a glance in her direction. "Meaning you and me?"

She nodded primly, relieved she had managed to get that out. She was beginning to employ bravado, but inside, she was still uneasy and nervous no matter what sort of outer demeanor she was trying to maintain.

"At least to start with, yes," she answered, her words finally managing to come out after making their way over a bone-dry tongue.

Sam put his key into the ignition. They had to be getting back. *He* had to be getting back. "You're volunteering?"

She squared her shoulders even as the car began to move forward. "Yes."

Did she have *any* idea what she was letting herself get into? "To read letters most likely written by psychopaths?"

She needed to focus on the positive aspects of what they were going to be doing, not what was most likely actually going to be in the letters. Exercising extreme mental control, she could separate herself from that aspect.

"If it winds up saving one life," she told him, "sure. What's a queasy stomach in exchange for someone's life?"

Sam found himself laughing, more in disbelief than from the dark humor of the situation. And maybe, just maybe, he was a little pleased as well, pleased that she could be so strong when she looked so fragile.

"You really are something else, aren't you, Zoe?" he responded.

She really wasn't sure just what Sam meant by that. But asking him to explain might destroy the magic of the moment. And, right now, he had made her feel special even if he hadn't intended for that to happen.

"Just a responsible citizen who doesn't want to see any more bloodshed," she replied simply.

"You might regret that choice," Sam predicted.

She raised her head just a little as she drew her shoulders back, a soldier about to walk into a battle with an unknown enemy. "I doubt it."

The corners of Sam's mouth curved just a little.

We'll see, Zoe. We'll see.

Although Sam really would have rather talked her out of it for her own sake, there was no denying that he could certainly use Zoe's help wading through Matthew's prized possessions.

They were currently even more shorthanded than

usual at the station. They had never been what could even remotely be termed "overstaffed" and there were two of their people out with the flu. While neither the officer nor the detective who were out sick were particularly the sharpest knives in the proverbial drawer, they were still useful in their own way.

Right now, laid up and in bed, they weren't being useful at all.

Walking ahead of Zoe into the bullpen where both the officers and the detectives of the Granite Gulch police force did their paperwork, Sam led the way to where his desk was located.

All the desks were arranged in twos and faced one another, except for his and Jim Murray's, the police chief's. The police chief's desk was all the way on the other side of the room, in a place where he could oversee everyone else.

Sam put the box down on top of his desk, right next to the refurbished computer the department had assigned him.

"Okay, you can sit here, on the other side of my desk," he said, indicating the long, narrow table that butted up against his desk. It doubled as a catchall table. "I'd put you at Riley's desk," he said, referring to the detective who was out sick, "but it hasn't been cleaned since the station opened and I don't want you catching anything."

Sam, she realized by the expression on his face, was only half kidding.

He brought over one of the empty chairs and positioned it at the table. Her chair faced his.

"This okay?" he asked her.

All she had to do was look up to see him. She couldn't think of a better view.

"Perfect," she responded.

"I wouldn't go that far," Sam muttered.

Turning back to the box he'd opened, he dug into it and extracted all the letters. He deposited them on the desk, tossing the box down beside his wastepaper basket.

The letters were written on all kinds of paper, from scented stationary, to sheets that looked as if they had been torn out of yellowed journals, to pages that had emerged out of state-of-the-art printers. They were handwritten, they were typed and some were comprised of letters that were cut out of other sources and pasted on the page.

Those, Sam assumed, were threatening letters rather than letters penned in admiration. Once they were ruled as threatening letters, they automatically found their way to the bottom of the pile.

Zoe took in the resulting stacks. At first glance, the job of sifting through them seemed almost overwhelming. But, like every other job, this could be effectively tackled one piece at a time.

When she turned to face Sam, she had her gung ho expression on.

"I could separate them into different piles," she volunteered.

He wasn't sure what she meant. "What kind of piles? You mean by size?"

Zoe shook her head, the loose blond wisps, he noticed, almost moving independently of her motion. He blocked the urge to reach out and touch the loose strands, to tuck them behind her ears.

"No, by type." She broke it up into the broadest categories. "You know, love letters, letters expressing admiration and the desire to follow in his path, letters that promise hell and damnation are waiting for him for all his heinous deeds. Type," she repeated.

"Probably not too many of those," Sam predicted. "And in order for you to do that," he went on to point out, "you'd have to give each letter at least a quick once-over. Might as well save yourself the time and trouble and just read them straight through.

"When we finish each letter," he suggested, "that's when we can separate them. That way, we can see how many we have in each category once we're done. With luck, we'll find the guy we're looking for in the 'wannabe' pile," he speculated.

"Okay," Zoe readily agreed, eager to get started. The sooner they started, the sooner they would be done with it. "Sounds like a plan."

But as Zoe picked up her first pile of letters, Sam put his hand on her wrist, stopping her for a moment. "You're sure you're up to this?" he asked again. He was trying to remain indifferent, but concern kept poking through the layers he'd wrapped around himself.

"I'm a librarian," she reminded him and there was

a touch of pride in her voice. "Reading is second nature to me."

Sam frowned as his eyes met hers. "You know what I mean."

He found her smile almost radiant—the next moment, it struck him as odd that he would even come up with that image.

"Yes, I know, and thank you for asking, but I'll be fine," she told him. "You'd be surprised what I've come across."

"Maybe you can tell me sometime," Sam said absently. His mind was already elsewhere as he began to read the top letter in his stack.

"Maybe," Zoe agreed under her breath.

Settling in, Zoe got started.

She decided a couple of hours later it was, all in all, like exploring the underbelly of the social misfits and depraved.

She read letters written by clearly troubled women who vividly described fantasies they created in their minds about what they either wanted to do to Matthew, or have him do to them. Some of the things were pretty graphic. All were appalling. Each woman ended her letter declaring undivided love and the hope that she and Matthew would someday be united by the bonds of matrimony.

Each and every one of them left a terrible taste in her mouth.

Sam was far more vocal about the ones he read than she was.

"What kind of a crazy woman wants to marry a serial killer?" he demanded, having to restrain himself from balling up and throwing the letter he had just read into the trash.

"A lonely one," Zoe answered simply.

He raised his eyes to her, surprised she would say anything in the writer's defense. "Doesn't this revolt you?" he wanted to know.

"Yes," Zoe readily admitted with feeling. There was no doubt about that. However, she had something to add. "But it also makes me sad."

"Sad?" he questioned incredulously. "Why?"

"Because it takes a deep, penetrating loneliness to want to be with someone who's killed so many people. It's like the women who write these letters feel they don't deserve any better." She sighed and then looked at Sam. "Think how awful they must feel inside."

"So you *feel* for them?" he questioned. He couldn't begin to understand how someone as normal as Zoe could empathize with the unhinged women who were writing these letters.

Zoe didn't give him a direct reply. Instead, she said, "Think how terrible it is to get to that state, where you feel no one cares, no one will ever care, and this is the best you can hope for, to get a convicted, insane serial killer to marry you."

Sam snorted. Her heart was too soft. "You ask me, they should all be locked up."

"It would probably be safer that way," she agreed. "But maybe if someone had just taken the time to listen to them years ago—"

He had an entirely different suggestion in mind. Leaning across his desk, he reached for the remaining pile of letters in front of Zoe. "Maybe you shouldn't read any more."

Zoe drew the stacks back out of his reach before he could take them away. "You asked me a question. I just answered it. From now on, I'll keep my opinion to myself," she promised, picking up another letter.

Sam shook his head and sank down in his chair. He moved it so the chair was back to its original position. After a minute, he got back to the business of reading.

But he had to admit, despite everything else going on, Zoe continued to intrigue him.

Chapter 12

Sam leaned back in his chair. It creaked in protest even as he rotated his neck from side to side, trying to loosen the stiffness he felt.

He couldn't remember the last time he had put in so many hours sitting at his desk, surrounded by paper. His body felt tense and his state of mind was in an even worse place.

Feeling as if he couldn't read another sentence, much less another letter today, Sam pushed himself back from his desk, as if putting space between himself and the letters would somehow help both his state of mind and his body.

"I don't know about you, but I could certainly stand to take a long, cleansing shower right about now. Reading these letters dissolved any lingering shred of hope I had left for humanity."

Not that there had exactly been an abundance of hope in his life to begin with, he thought.

When he received no response from Zoe, he looked up in her direction.

"Zoe?"

When he actually focused in on her face, he was surprised to see there were tears spilling down her cheeks.

She was crying.

Sam bit off a curse, refraining from saying out loud the words that instantly sprang to his tongue. No matter how annoyed or angry he was, gut instincts curbed his tongue. Zoe wasn't the kind of person people cursed around. It just didn't seem right.

But there was nothing preventing him from letting his anger come through.

"I knew it. I knew I shouldn't have let you help read these letters."

Getting up, he circumvented his own desk and came around to the long table on her side.

But when he tried to take the letter she was reading away from her, Zoe wouldn't let him. She surprised him by holding on to it.

"Zoe, give me the letter," he told her. It was an order not a request, even though he tried not to bark out the words.

Instead of surrendering the letter, Zoe looked up at him, tears still shimmering in her eyes.

He felt something tighten in his stomach. Hard. He'd long since stopped being aware of any protective instinct he might have once possessed. That was gone, except perhaps, in some small way, in the case of his family. But even that occurred in moderation.

However, there was something about Zoe, about the deeply sad look he saw in her eyes, that seemed to rouse that dormant gut feeling, woke it up and brought it to the surface.

"Zoe?"

There were a hundred questions woven into that one salutation and he waited for her to respond to at least one of them. That he could wait and not just forge ahead to do what he wanted to surprised him. Zoe seemed to draw out responses from him that he had no idea even existed within him.

She drew in a very shaky breath and, being Zoe, the first thing she did was apologize. "I'm sorry. I didn't mean to cry, it's just that…"

"That what?" he prodded, trying his best not to sound as impatient as he was to get some kind of an answer that made sense out of her.

Impatient with herself—she didn't want to add to the burden that Sam was carrying by acting like a scatterbrained, weepy woman—Zoe wiped away the telltale streaks on her cheeks with the back of her hand and did her best to answer him in a normal voice, not one choked with tears that had welled up in her throat.

"There are letters from the relatives of the victims mixed in with the so-called 'fan' letters and marriage proposals," she explained.

Those had to be what Matthew had been referring to when he'd said that some of the letters were "ugly," Sam thought. Matthew would have regarded anything that would have made an attempt to make him feel guilty or cowardly as "ugly."

"Those are so heartbreaking," Zoe told him, her voice swelling with emotion again. "Some of the people writing to him are clearly trying to make Matthew feel guilty, but mostly the people writing the letters talk about how the world is an emptier place now that he's taken away the most important person in their lives." There was an innocent need to know in her eyes as she raised them to his, Sam thought. "How can he live with himself, Sam? Knowing he's responsible for so much misery, how can that man live with himself?"

Sam shrugged. He really wished he had a good answer for that, but all he could do was tell her the only thing that occurred to him.

"Easy," he replied, his voice flat, scrubbed free of any feeling. "It's the only way Matthew could have gotten any sort of notoriety and being famous seems to be extremely important to him, never mind for what," Sam concluded.

Zoe couldn't begin to understand someone like that. And because she couldn't relate, the serial killer's actions made no sense to her.

"He's as empty and as broken as all these other people who have been writing to him," Zoe said.

"That's dear old Dad," Sam said, a sharp bitterness slicing through his tone. And then he looked at her, a slight smile forming on his lips. “You catch on fast, kid,” he told her, nodding his approval. He got back to what he’d started to say earlier. “Tell you what, we’ve been at this way too long today. I think we both need to take a major break before I bring you home.”

He planned to pick up something to eat on his way home and he didn’t think it fair that Zoe should have to cook for herself after all the time she’d put in working with him today.

“What do you say to grabbing some dinner at the Blackthorn County All Night Diner?” he proposed.

She would have said yes to standing on a corner, eating day-old earthworms as long as it was with him. It wasn’t the food, it was the company that meant everything to her.

So, in response to his question, Zoe flashed a quick smile of thanks and answered, “Sure,” not trusting herself to say anything further at the moment without gracelessly putting her foot in her mouth. “Sounds like a good idea,” she agreed.

But before they left the station, Sam took the stacks of letters from her desk and his and placed the ones that had already been read into the box, while the others that still needed to be read were placed into the drawer by themselves.

Putting the box into a deeper side drawer, Sam locked both drawers, testing them to make sure they were secure before he pocketed the keys.

“Keeping your word to your father?” she asked,

clearly surprised as well as pleased to see what he was doing. Sam was one of the good guys despite his hardened facade, she thought.

"Keeping the evidence from being stolen and posted on the internet by some half-witted, enterprising idiot out to make a buck," Sam corrected. He wasn't one of those people who took credit where none was due.

"Here?" she asked, looking at Sam incredulously. They were at the police station. She would have thought things would have been safe here.

He was surprised that he found her naïveté almost sweet. Under ordinary circumstances, it should have irritated him.

"One thing I learned a long time ago," he told her as they walked out of the building, "you never know where temptation will take a person."

He was just finding that out on a personal level and he was doing what he could to keep that very new, very untried feeling that had reared its head in his chest under wraps as well as lock and key. He had a crime to solve and a riddle to unravel. That left him absolutely no time to explore anything outside of that, especially something that had come up out of nowhere and in such an untimely fashion.

"I think we can rule out the victims' relatives who wrote to him," Zoe said as they walked into the diner a few minutes later. "I don't see any one of them going on a rampage, killing innocent girls as a way of getting even with Matthew. I think if any of them had actually wanted to use murder as a way of getting even with the old man, they wouldn't have killed a bunch of strangers, they would have tried to kill someone in his family."

Sam laughed, shaking his head at her theory. Spotting an empty booth at the rear of the diner, he led the way there.

"If they'd done that," he said once he and Zoe had reached the booth, "they would have been sorely disappointed." Sam waited until she took her seat, then he slid into the booth on his side. "The old man doesn't give a—flying fig," he said, substituting the term at the last minute for the one he would have ordinarily used, "about any one of us."

"Maybe not then," Zoe qualified, slanting a glance at him as she let her sentence drift off.

"Maybe not ever," he corrected sharply.

Zoe held fast to her theory of why Matthew was dispensing clues in the manner he'd chosen. She was convinced she was right.

"If that was true, he wouldn't be spreading the clues out the way he is, saying he's going to dole out one each to you and your brothers and sister if you came to see him one at a time. My guess is that seeing you all at once would probably overwhelm him and he wouldn't be able to make amends—"

She was a sweet and apparently innocent kid, but she had this all wrong, Sam thought.

He had to take the air out of her balloon, he decided, before she let it carry her away too far.

"The end of the world'll come before that man tries to make amends," he told her flatly.

"All right, not amends," Zoe conceded. "A connection, then. The man's broken inside, Sam, and reconnecting with his kids—"

Again, he had to put her straight. He really wished the world was as pure, as sugarcoated as Zoe saw it, but it wasn't.

"To reconnect, Matthew would have had to have been connected to us at some point, and that man *never* made any attempt to connect with any one of us at any time and that includes before, and *during*, his serial killer spree. The old man was always a lone wolf, an island unto himself. Other than his DNA, we never shared any part of him at any time."

She looked at Sam for a long moment. He might not look it, but right now, the man was like a stone wall and beating her head against it wasn't going to get her anywhere.

"You're determined not to let him in, aren't you?" she said quietly.

About to answer, Sam paused as the waitress came to take their order. He knew his by heart. This was where he came when hunger interfered with his work. Here and the Granite Gulch Bar and Saloon, but he only hit the latter after his shift was over.

Before giving his order to the waitress, he paused

and looked at Zoe. "You know what you want, or do you need some more time?"

Zoe surrendered the menu to the waitress. "I know what I want," she said, looking at Sam rather than the woman.

After the waitress left, promising to return with their meals shortly, Sam resumed the conversation that had been put on hold.

"I'm more open to letting lice into my life than letting in that old man. I'm playing his game to find my mother and to find a killer, not to find some kind of so-called resolution. I realized a long time ago that with him, there's no such thing."

She wasn't nearly as sure as he was, but then, she hadn't lived through what he had, either. So all she allowed herself to ask Sam was a strictly neutral question. "And you're okay with that?"

Incredibly, the waitress was back, placing their orders before them. They'd both ordered the same thing: cheeseburgers with fries. The only difference was that Zoe's came with a slice of tomato, as well.

"I'm more than okay with that," Sam said once they were alone again. "Now eat that damn hamburger before it gets cold, hard and tasteless. This place isn't exactly at the top of the list for home cooking," he commented darkly.

He came here because it was familiar, it was close and the prices were reasonable. What it amounted to, he knew, was that he came here by default, but he had never been one to be picky.

She'd struck a nerve and she knew it. She deliberately backed down. If Sam didn't care about his father the way he claimed he didn't, he wouldn't have reacted as quickly as he had to her suggestion about the man's motives.

There was still that little boy living somewhere within the gruff, tough man sitting opposite her in the dingy diner, she was sure of it.

Zoe told herself that somehow, some way, she had to find a way to reach him and help him heal, if only because of the fact that she couldn't stand to see Sam in pain. Even if she didn't see it in the way he conducted himself, there would have been no other conclusion to reach. Anyone who had lived through what he had clearly had to be in ongoing pain.

It wasn't until he brought Zoe home an hour later that another idea, completely out of left field, occurred to him.

He paused by her front door, examining the idea. "We've been going at this as if the person who killed Celia was a disciple of Matthew's," he told her, his voice growing more agitated as he spoke each word. "What if we're wrong?"

"Wrong?" she echoed. Since when did he admit to being wrong? "What do you mean?"

"What if whoever killed her was someone Celia knew?" Sam asked. The more he spoke, the more plausible his theory seemed to him. "Maybe a jealous ex-boyfriend getting revenge because she dumped him."

"Why the red bull's-eye?" Zoe wanted to know before she even commented on his initial idea. "How does that fit in?"

Sam shrugged. He certainly hadn't worked out any of the details. He was still feeling his way around.

"Maybe to throw us off," he guessed. As he talked out his theory, bits and pieces began to come together for him. "She was supposed to be marrying me. It wouldn't have taken much for someone to find out about the rotten branch on my family tree. Matthew created one hell of a stir in his day. Made life a living hell for the rest of us," he couldn't help commenting. "His story followed us no matter where we went.

"It took a lot of hard work to live that down," he recalled bitterly. "Maybe whoever killed Celia did a little digging and came up with this sick plot to throw the investigation off his trail." It didn't sound all that farfetched to him.

Zoe apparently agreed. "It's certainly worth looking into," she said. "But what about the other two victims? Why would he kill them?"

Those were some of the details he still needed to work out. "Maybe to throw us off—or maybe he didn't kill them. Someone else did and Celia's killer just took advantage of the pattern that was emerging." He looked at Zoe to see if she had any glaring objections to that. "There're lots of ways to play this."

And they were only multiplying by the moment, he couldn't help adding silently.

"You're going to need more help," Zoe concluded quietly, even as her mind raced to make plans and get things to fall into place. "I'll take a leave of absence from the library. In light of what's happened to my sister, they can't exactly turn me down. Besides, I do have a lot of vacation coming to me if they try to be sticklers about the request."

"I was just thinking the exact opposite," he told her. When Zoe looked at him quizzically, he said, "That maybe you should stop helping me. I don't want anything happening to you. You'll be safer if you're working at the library."

"I'd be safer if I was working next to you," she insisted. Because she could see he didn't agree, she argued, "I'd have a police detective right there, looking out for me."

Sam sighed deeply, irritated. "You know, for an easygoing woman, you're really damn stubborn."

She couldn't help smiling at his assessment, even though her answer was completely serious. "I found out that people step on you if you don't hold your ground and stand up for yourself. It's something I learned from Celia," she confessed.

"Yeah, and look how that worked out for her," he said pointedly. He hadn't said it to hurt her, although he suspected it might. He'd said it to scare Zoe into backing off.

He should have known better.

Zoe surprised him when she responded, "You said stubborn, not greedy."

Sam let the matter drop, at least the part about convincing her to back off. But not the idea that someone in Celia's life had been the reason why it had ended so abruptly.

"Can you draw up a list of Celia's past boyfriends for me?" he asked Zoe.

"Well, there were guys," Zoe admitted, thinking back over her older sister's rather tumultuous dating life. "But most of them didn't last more than a few weeks or so. Maybe even a month, but not much longer than that. She'd either get bored, or find someone who sparked her interest more, usually because they were richer.

"But there was this one guy who kept coming back," Zoe suddenly remembered, growing more animated. "Celia would get back with him every time she was between men." Zoe stopped, hesitating, as she looked at Sam. She couldn't help thinking how this had to sound to him. "You sure you want to hear this?"

"You're not hurting my feelings if that's what you're thinking," he assured her. "I'm long past having my feelings hurt when it comes to your sister. What was this boomerang's name?"

She didn't have to pause. She remembered. Celia had actually mentioned him the day she died.

"Johnny Vine," Zoe said. "She used to make jokes about the way he'd hang on, like some kind of a 'clinging vine.'"

"That couldn't have been good for his ego," Sam commented, thinking maybe that could have been motive enough.

"I don't know much about him," Zoe confessed. "Just that he was into something shady. And—" Zoe stopped, hesitating before she continued.

"What?" Sam asked sharply.

"Just before Celia told me that she was tricking you into marrying her, she laughed and said she wouldn't be surprised if Johnny crashed the wedding and tried to win her back by dragging her away from the church at gunpoint."

Real winner, Sam thought. "That meant he had a gun," Sam concluded out loud, looking to Zoe for confirmation.

Zoe nodded. "She mentioned something about it. Said he liked showing off, proving how good he was with it." She paused, berating herself for not having remembered all this earlier. It was almost as if her brain had been paralyzed. "Do you think he did it?"

"I think it's worth looking into. I'll see what I can dig up on him in the morning. In the meantime, you get some sleep."

Because she'd been so relentless in trying to help, Sam bent over and kissed her forehead.

It was meant as a brotherly gesture—and just possibly—intended to negate the last physical contact he'd initiated with her, the one that had been *less* than brotherly.

When his lips left her forehead, Zoe looked up at him. No words passed her lips.

They didn't have to.

Chapter 13

Sam felt something.

He actually *felt* something, he realized. And that was bad.

Bad because feelings led to a loss of judgment. Feelings made people do things they shouldn't, forget what was important, forget the principles they had always lived by. Feelings clouded a person's true perception of things and made instant fools out of normally intelligent people.

Feeling something for someone was seductive, created a rush that, if large enough and fast enough, could temporarily—and completely—blot out the immediate world.

And he couldn't afford to let any of that happen.

And yet—

And yet, he could feel himself standing on the edge of a precipice, wavering. Being irresistibly drawn to a place he had no business, no *right* to go.

While he fought this brutal, internal war that encompassed all of about a minute even as it felt as if it was embracing eternity, he heard Zoe ask, "Would you like to come inside for a minute?"

The words had rushed out almost breathlessly. She knew she couldn't have gotten them out any other way. She was being brazen, going for the brass ring, accepting the fact that if she got Sam to herself at all, it was merely by default.

Because he was so weary.

Because he needed someone just for the night and she was the only one there.

But that was all right.

Someone else would have upbraided her and told her she was selling herself short, but the way she saw it, she wasn't selling herself at all. She was finally getting what she had always, *always* longed for.

A night with Sam.

Sam, who had filled her heart from the very first moment she had ever seen him. Sam, whom she truly felt she had been born loving. If it was one-sided, okay, so be it. She accepted that.

As long as she could be there with him, breathing the same air, helping him battle his demons, she was happy. It was exactly what she wanted to do and where she wanted to be.

Making love with Sam—if it came to that—would only be the huge sparkling bow on a gift she never dreamed she would actually ever get.

Zoe unlocked her door and opened it a crack.

Yes, he wanted to come in, Sam thought. More than anything, he wanted to follow Zoe inside, close the door and just for a little while, shed the agony that seemed to always drape over him like some sort of heavy metal net, covering him from top to bottom.

But that wouldn't be fair to Zoe.

He didn't want to be like the monster that was his father, didn't want to be guilty of only thinking of himself.

He'd almost willed himself to leave…

And then he felt her fingers slipping through his, saw her turning slightly toward the door. She pushed it open and then she was drawing him behind her as she stepped over the threshold into her house.

"I should be going," he told her, although it was clear his heart wasn't in the protest he'd voiced reluctantly.

Zoe pretended she hadn't heard him.

"Would you like something to drink?" she offered, butterflies doing an aerial assault inside her stomach. "I've got some wine, some coffee and some kind of soda in the refrigerator, I think. And there's always water," she added with a smile she was certain appeared nervous around the edges.

"I'm not thirsty," he told her.

Sam knew he should just turn around and leave. It was the smart, not to mention the safe, thing for him to do. But he just couldn't seem to take his eyes off her, as if looking at Zoe would finally enable him to see the world more clearly.

"Hungry, maybe?" Zoe asked, trying again. And then she flushed, embarrassed. "No, we just ate, why would you be hungry? Never mind," she said, trying to dismiss her nervous error.

"Yes."

The word had come out in almost a whisper, uttered so softly she barely heard Sam.

Leaning in, she asked almost hesitantly, "What did you say?"

"Yes," he repeated, saying the word more loudly this time. "I am."

"You are," she said, slightly confused. And then, suddenly, she realized what he was saying yes to, or thought she did. "You're hungry?"

The look in his eyes told her they were no longer on the topic of food.

The smile she felt radiated into her eyes a second before it found its way to her lips.

Zoe took a half step closer to him.

That was all it took.

The next second, his arms were around her, holding her to him. Less than a heartbeat after that, his mouth was on hers and every wall he had so carefully erected between himself and everyone else in the rest of the world instantly crumbled, disintegrating like so many grains of dry sand that surrendered themselves to the wind.

She felt fluid in his arms, not as if she had just melted at his touch, but like silk ribbons caught up and dancing in the warm summer breeze.

His blood heated at the very thought of possessing her, of having her. Had she been someone else, one of the faceless, nameless women who had passed through his life in years gone by without leaving a trace, he would have taken her then and there, made love with her and left, all within an hour's time, if that long.

But this was Zoe and that evoked a tenderness within him that superseded the devastating need eating away at him.

So he kept himself in check every single step of the way. He forced himself to attempt something new. Rather than give in to the raging urgency of his desire, Sam reined it in and proceeded to seduce Zoe in stages, making love to every part of her before he made love with the whole of her.

And, in so doing, he seduced not only her, but himself, as well. And, he realized too late, he had never really been seduced before. Not like this. He'd never allowed himself to feel enthralled—and yet, that was exactly what Zoe did to him, exactly the way she made him feel.

Rather than roughly separate her from her clothing, Sam coaxed the garments from her body, teasing buttons apart, moving material slowly aside. Exposing more and more to his gaze, but doing so a little at a time. And in so doing, he unconsciously wound up ensnaring himself as firmly as if he had lain on the ground and been covered from head to toe with ropes, the mighty giant Gulliver being taken and all but gift wrapped by the tiny, determined Lilliputians.

Zoe had woven her magic around him just by being, he realized as he kissed her over and over again, heating her body just as surely as he was heating his own.

The ache she felt grew to almost overwhelming proportions.

At twenty-four, Zoe had never been with anyone. There'd been one clumsy attempt while she was still in college, but she had lost her nerve—not to mention she'd felt disgusted at her partner's less than skillful groping—and bolted before anything of any consequence had happened between them.

As a result, she began thinking of herself as cold, frigid, and doomed to be left out of what everyone else seemed to be celebrating: romantic unions.

Or at least that was what it seemed like to her, because the subject of love, of physical gratification, was in every second song, every second movie and in just about every single communication that was going on around her.

The men she interacted with, both at work and in her daily life, did nothing for her, caused no temporary flights of fantasy, no momentary longings or spontaneous daydreams.

But even being within a few feet of Sam, with just the hint of possible lovemaking, had caused things to begin happening inside of her, created incredibly strong longings to take hold of her, to urge her on and make her bolder than she had ever been in her life.

Which was why she had all but thrown herself at him and had felt absolutely no remorse at doing so.

And even now, there were no second thoughts, no misgivings or inner hesitation.

There was only joy.

Wildly overwhelming, boundless joy because of what she was feeling for this man. Not to mention an excitement the likes of which she didn't recall ever encountering. Her whole body felt as if it was poised, waiting for something wondrous to happen.

And she could feel the anticipation building within her, growing stronger, bigger, more intense. If she were a train, she would have sworn she was building up a full head of steam, because it felt just like that.

But different.

And then, suddenly, out of nowhere, this explosion—it was the only thing she could liken it to—detonated within her, causing her to internally scramble *toward* the sensation in order to absorb every single shred of it. That was when she realized she had all but levitated off the sofa—they had somehow managed to find their way over to it, although for the life of her, she had no idea when or how.

The inner explosion, she realized now, had occurred in response to something wondrous Sam had done to her with his hands, his breath and his mouth. Rather than be embarrassed—something she would have thought a normal response from her under any other circumstances—she was thrilled beyond words. So thrilled that her body was fairly vibrating from the effects.

Humming, actually.

Was this what she had been missing out on by not making love with someone?

But then, Zoe knew in her heart that what she was experiencing was only wondrous because she was experiencing it with Sam, the man she had surrendered her soul to years ago. Being with someone else wouldn't have had this sort of an effect on her and she knew it. She believed that with her entire heart.

And then, just as she was certain it couldn't possibly get any better, Sam moved over her—his body hovering just over hers—and, capturing her mouth, he began to unite them for the final culmination.

But as he entered her, the unexpected flash of pain that went through her extremity had her involuntarily wincing.

The movement, as well as the resistance he met, was enough to alert him.

Sam began to draw back and she knew that once he did, it would be over. He'd turn from her and leave her and maybe, because of that, he'd never be back, not to talk to her, certainly not to come close to doing what they'd just been doing.

So rather than accept what was about to happen, rather than be in submission the way she had been for so much of her life, Zoe rebelled. She wouldn't let him withdraw. Instead, she arched up against him, forcing Sam to suspend his withdrawal.

Not only that, but she began to move urgently against him, ignoring the pain this physical union had created until it ceased to exist.

The only thing that mattered was that Sam didn't turn away from her, didn't stop making love with her. She wanted to at least have this one evening unmarred by rejection.

To hold it to her when all the empty nights that would follow came.

So she did what her instincts prompted her to do and in so doing, she made love to Sam until he was forced to make love *with* her.

He wasn't strong enough to stop, not when she held him prisoner like this.

Despite all his control, all his logic and common sense, he discovered he was no match for Zoe's determination. And just like that, he succumbed, giving in to the wants and needs she had stirred and woken up inside of him.

His mouth covering hers, his body pressed against her until someone standing ten feet away couldn't have been able to identify where one of them ended and the other one began, Sam let go and allowed himself to move, unrestricted, to the wild, primitive dance he heard in his head.

The one he felt in his body.

The tempo increased, the music played faster, harder, and he went with it until suddenly, he and

Zoe were diving off the highest peak in this incredible new world that had been created by just the two of them.

His arms tightened around her so hard, neither one of them could breathe for a moment.

And then the descent came languidly, depositing them back to the ground. Back to earth and everything that was around them to create this one, common earth they both knew.

With the ebbing of euphoria came the full realization of just what had happened. What *he* had done to her that could never be undone.

"You're a virgin," Sam said, his voice sounding almost accusatory.

Please, please don't ruin this. Don't get angry or say something I'm going to regret.

"Was," she corrected. "I *was* a virgin. Until just a little while ago."

He ignored her attempt to joke him out of the seriousness of the topic he had raised. "Why didn't you *tell* me?"

"How was I supposed to work that into any conversation you and I ever had?" she wanted to know, then reminded him, "There weren't all that many of them, if you recall."

Frustration—with himself, not her—wove itself through every word he uttered. "You should have told me tonight, before we got started."

She raised her eyes to his. "Then we wouldn't have gotten started, would we?" Zoe challenged.

Exasperation laced itself through his frustration. "I didn't say that."

"You didn't have to. It's there in your eyes." Taking a breath, she struggled to keep the tears at bay until after he left her. "I'm sorry I turned out to be such a disappointment," she told him, apologizing for her inexperience. She took it to be the reason why he was so annoyed now.

"I didn't say *that*," he stressed.

He didn't have to, she thought. Everything about his manner now said it for him. But holding on to a sliver of hope that just maybe she actually was wrong, Zoe asked, "Then why are you mad?"

"Because, damn it, your first time's supposed to be different."

He could have been gentler, kinder, Sam upbraided himself. He could have picked a better time, a better location—or better yet, he could have left her alone altogether, to have her first time with someone else, someone whose soul wasn't as wounded as his was. She deserved the best and that wasn't him.

"It was," she told him softly. Lifting a hand, she touched his face. "Different than anything I could have imagined."

"Your first time should have been with someone special," he bit off, "not me."

"Someone special *is* you," Zoe insisted, whispering the words.

He felt a million things at that moment. Mostly he felt unworthy. But he couldn't resist saying, with a touch of humor, “You really know how to play hard to get, don’t you?”

Before she could frame an answer, he pulled her back under him and allowed himself to get lost in her just one more time.

In all honesty, he had no other choice. He wanted her too much and she had completely undone him with that look in her eyes. She saw him the way he wanted to be, not the way he knew he was.

Chapter 14

Long after the lovemaking had ceased and the euphoria it had created slipped into the shadows, Sam lay awake, listening to the woman beside him breathe.

Things had been stirred within him tonight, things that were better off left dormant. His life had become streamlined, especially now that he wasn't getting married, wasn't going to be a father with a child to round things out.

What just happened tonight brought a third dimension into his two dimensional life. He wasn't sure if he could handle that. And he was better off, he thought, if he didn't even try.

He waited until he thought Zoe was asleep, and then he quietly slipped out of her bed.

He was still somewhat astounded they had made love two more times tonight, winding up in her bed the last time strictly because she had asked him to make love with her there.

He felt he owed that to her. To give in to the small request, seeing as how she'd turned his whole world upside down and made him feel, just for a little while, as if he was just a normal guy. As if he wasn't being weighed down by the vast amount of baggage he had been dragging around in his wake for so long.

Dressing as quickly as he could without making a single sound, Sam picked up his shoes, ready to tiptoe out to the front door before he put them on and risk making any noise that could, inadvertently, wake Zoe up.

But just as he was about to leave, Sam couldn't resist just one more moment with her.

Bending over, he lightly brushed his lips against her forehead.

He couldn't help thinking that was how it had all started tonight and somehow, it seemed fitting it was the way it ended, as well.

As he turned away and headed out of the bedroom, he didn't see Zoe smile to herself, didn't know that this one single act of tenderness on his part put an entirely different light on his leaving her this way.

Zoe watched him leave through eyes that were closed down to narrow slits, then hugged her pillow to her.

It was all good, she thought. Whatever happened next, this was all good.

Sam went in early the next day. He had a serial killer to catch and a possible new lead to follow up on.

He wasn't prepared for what was waiting for him at his desk.

Zoe.

The takeout coffee he had picked up on his way to the station nearly slipped from his fingers and that would have added a new black coat of thick sludge to the already aged, cracked flooring.

"What are you doing here?" he demanded gruffly.

Questions crowded his mind. Was she going to say anything about the way he had left her without a word last night? Was she here to tell him last night had brought a new dynamic between them that he had to take into account now?

"Reading the letters you brought back from prison," Zoe answered simply, her quiet manner temporarily shooting holes through all his uneasy questions and his even more uneasy reaction to seeing her here. "I didn't finish my stack yesterday."

And then he realized something else.

"But I left all the letters locked in my desk," he protested.

Even as he pointed it out, Sam covered his left pocket, feeling for the keys he'd deposited into it. They were still there.

Zoe smiled up at him brightly, looking as if her explanation was simplicity personified. "I used to get locked out of my desk at the library a lot. One of the students who came in to do research on a regular basis for his PhD paper felt sorry for me and showed me a trick using a nail file and a long, thin nail—like the kind used to hang up pictures, not the kind found at the end of your finger," she clarified. "It doesn't hurt the lock," she promised, glancing at the desk drawer she had unlocked.

Sam shook his head as he sank down at his desk. The chair's creak of protest hardly registered.

"You keep amazing me," he confessed.

It only made her smile widen. He forced himself to look away. Otherwise, he wasn't going to be able to focus on his work.

Sam nodded at the stack of letters she had on the table before her. "Find anything?"

Zoe shook her head, obviously frustrated. "Not yet. A few more letters from the relatives of his victims, but most of the others either want to have his baby, or be just like him, but confess they don't have his—" she paused for a moment before saying, "let's call it guts," she decided, not wanting to use the actual word she found in a lot of the letters.

"You ask me, he was totally gutless, taking out his shortcomings and insecurities on men who looked like my uncle because he couldn't accomplish anything worthwhile on his own," Sam told her bitterly. His words echoing back to him, Sam stopped and collected himself. He couldn't let himself go off on that track. Nothing would get done, then. "Since you're here, why don't you go on reading those letters, see if anything pops out at you?"

His tone of voice alerted her. "You sound like you're going to be doing something else."

"I'm going to see if I can come up with some kind of a connection between this Johnny Vine character you brought up last night and the other two women who were recently murdered." Since she looked interested, he continued to explain a little of his procedure. "I thought I'd start by cross-referencing the files, see if his name pops up in either one of the victims' lives. Or if I can find any sort of a connection between the two women and your sister."

She noticed he didn't refer to Celia by name, or mention anything about her having been his fiancée. She assumed it was deliberate.

That was a chapter of his life better left closed, she thought, until such time—if ever—that Sam could deal with the lie he'd been fed by her sister in order to get him to agree to marry her.

"Sounds good," Zoe agreed as she went back to reading the letters in the stack in front of her.

He paused a moment, looking at her as Zoe picked up the first letter and began to read. "You don't have to agree with everything I say, you know."

"I know," she answered. "And I don't."

He'd yet to hear her really disagree with him, but he let that go. It would be better for both of them if he just did his job.

Stifling an exasperated noise, Sam leaned back in his chair, pushing it as far back as it could go without making him fall. He scrubbed his hands over his face, wishing, not for the first time, he could find some way to revitalize his flagging energy.

It was beginning to feel as if he had been going around in circles forever. Going around in circles and getting nowhere.

Zoe had sat quietly in her chair this entire time, reading letter after letter, making no comment about any of the contents she came across because she didn't want to disturb him. Some of it had turned her stomach. She took Sam's unintelligible noise now to mean he had either come to a dead end, or had opted to stop here and take a break.

Either way, the need for her self-imposed silence was over.

"Nothing?" she questioned, knowing he wouldn't have sounded that way if he'd triumphantly stumbled across a connection between the women and Johnny, or the women and her sister. The last she'd heard, none had existed between any of them. Not the women, not Johnny, but she was always hoping for miracles.

Last night should be enough of a miracle to satisfy you for a long, long time, a little voice in her head pointed out.

"Nothing," Sam said with disgusted finality as he slammed shut the top drawer he'd just opened purely for the satisfaction of having something to slam that wasn't breakable. His temper had already cost him enough over the past couple of years. It seemed that when it flared suddenly, frustration would take over and breaking something seemed to be a way to alleviate that pent-up feeling.

You're not a damn kid anymore, he upbraided himself. *Only kids have tantrums. Grow up, for God's sake.*

Sam blew out a breath and further elaborated, "No, no connection." He straightened up and pulled his chair back up to his desk.

"What's next?" she asked, curious. She wanted to be ready in case Sam suddenly jumped to his feet and took off.

"Next we bring him in for questioning, find out if somehow he fell through the cracks and he's actually got a history for some other awful crime," Sam answered, biting the words off.

He really hadn't expected it to be this easy, but once in a blue moon, things actually fell into place. Given his personal and professional background, he told himself he should really have known better.

"Maybe I should go through Celia's things at her condo," Zoe suggested, "see if I can find anything that might be useful. I've put it off because I wasn't up to looking through her things," she confessed, "but now that you think there's a chance we could find something that might point to her killer that way, I'll do it. I can go now," she volunteered, unconsciously squaring her shoulders as she started to get up.

"*We* can go now—or in a little while," Sam amended, stopping her in her tracks. "I've got a couple of things to look into first. You just keep on doing what you're doing," he told her as he rose to his feet.

"You're going to leave me behind, aren't you?" Zoe asked quietly.

Although she'd asked Sam the question, she really didn't need him to say anything. She already knew the answer.

The fact that she did—he could see it in her face—just about blew his mind. Just what the hell was going on here?

He stood there, as if his feet were suddenly glued to the floor, staring at Zoe in wonder. He wasn't transparent, so what was the deal here?

"What made you ask that?" he wanted to know.

"I'm also a student of body language—there's not all that much to do when you're a librarian," Zoe explained in almost an aside. "Your body language is very obvious. It says you're planning to take off the second you make it out of this room."

Sam sighed. So much for maintaining secrecy, something that had always been of tantamount importance to him, born of the days where everything he or his siblings did was taken apart and examined by an all-invasive public who thrived on dissecting the lives of people who had, through no fault of their own, been thrown into the public arena.

Since he was going to her sister's condo, maybe having Zoe there with him and the investigative team he was bringing with him would be useful. He'd only spent one night at Celia's place himself. Zoe undoubtedly knew where her sister kept things in her home far better than he did.

"C'mon," he told her with resignation. "If you're coming, let's go."

Zoe didn't need any more encouragement than that.

Sam expected to find some sort of a telltale clue amid Celia's things. Zoe expected to be of help to him. Neither one of them expected to find what they did once the door to the condo was unlocked.

"What the hell—? It looks like a hurricane went through here," Sam remarked, looking around the interior as he stepped across the threshold.

Nothing had been left standing in its original position.

Bookcases were emptied of their books, throw pillows that belonged on the sofa, or on the two beds in the bedrooms, along with upholstered cushions had their stuffing hacked out by someone who was very obviously searching for something and growing increasingly agitated the more that "something" apparently eluded him.

Sam turned to the small team of forensics investigators who were standing behind him at the condo's entrance and set them loose.

"See if you can figure out what it was that whoever ransacked this place was looking for. Maybe he missed it somehow, or at least left one of his prints behind. Maybe a partial print," he added.

None of those limited scenarios sounded very promising to him, but he had to at least appear to try to find something, had to authorize the thorough sweep of Celia's residence just in case there was something the killer overlooked or neglected to take with him.

"Can you think of anything this guy could have been looking for?" he asked, turning to Zoe.

She lifted her shoulders, then let them fall in a helpless shrug. "If this is Johnny's work and he went through Celia's things, looking for something, I don't think it would look this bad. I just can't see him being this desperate about anything. Celia could drive a person crazy," she readily agreed, "but this is a whole new level of crazy," Zoe commented, wading through the scattered debris. "Besides, the couple of times I saw him, Johnny seemed so laid-back, he could have made a turtle seem agitated and uptight in comparison."

The man didn't exactly sound like someone Celia would have had hanging around her, Sam thought. The woman he had known sought excitement, not boredom.

"Why would Celia be willing to have this guy come back into her life time and again, the way you indicated he did? What was the big attraction with this guy?" he wanted to know.

Zoe honestly had no real answer to that. She proceeded cautiously with the sliver of a theory she did have to offer. "Well, he's good-looking, but that definitely wouldn't have been enough for Celia."

He agreed with Zoe there. From what he'd come

to find out about the woman he'd almost unwittingly married, there was only one attraction for her.

"Was he well off?" he asked Zoe, making a mental note to look into the man's finances the first moment he had the opportunity to do so.

"There were times she said he threw money around," Zoe recalled. "But the last time I saw him with her, he looked like he was down to his last ten dollars, so my guess is the answer's no, he wasn't. Most likely, his way of 'earning' money wasn't really aboveboard. He really didn't strike me as the most savory character," she confessed to Sam.

As a matter of fact, now that she thought of it, outside of Sam, her sister's taste in men wasn't very good at all.

Sam stopped cautiously picking through the clothing that had been dumped out of Celia's dresser drawers and onto the floor. Rising back to his feet, he pocketed the handkerchief he'd used to not get his own prints on things although he knew they had to be here somewhere in the condo. After all, he had spent that one night here. He'd been drunk and probably drugged as well, but he'd still touched some things.

He was going to have to give his prints to the forensics investigators to rule him out, Sam thought. He walked back into the living room with Zoe close behind him. Damn, but this was a mess.

"I think it's time we hauled this guy in for questioning," Sam said, stopping to pick up a framed photograph that was lying, facedown, on the tiled floor. Flipping it over, he saw the glass was cracked and shattered in places.

It was the photograph he had grudgingly agreed to. It was taken at a studio of the two of them and had been the photograph sent to the local newspaper, announcing their engagement and upcoming wedding.

Staring at it, he still couldn't believe any of this—his involvement with Celia, the baby that first was, then wasn't there—had taken place.

He allowed the framed, now glassless photograph to fall onto the sofa.

When he looked up, he saw Zoe had been silently watching him. He had no idea what was going on in her mind, only that the look in her eyes was one filled with sympathy.

The woman just wasn't real, he thought. Anyone else would have either made some sort of a disparaging remark about her sister's underhanded ways, or asked something typical, like did he still, after all this, have any feelings for Celia?

At the very least, she might have attempted to sweep him mentally away from all this by bringing up what had gone down between them last night.

But Zoe had done none of these. She'd just given him his space.

And he was grateful, even if he didn't tell her.

"C'mon," he said. "There's nothing for us to find here. If there *is* anything, forensics will find it and get back to me. Do you know where this Johnny Vine lives?" he asked her.

Zoe shook her head. "Celia never said anything directly. She did mention he lived in town somewhere."

"Can't be too hard to find," Sam concluded. "The guy's got to have some kind of a paper trail available. Driver's license, credit card, something," he said as he led the way out of the chaotic condominium and past the forensics team.

Zoe was quick to join him, relieved to be getting out of the unsettling scene and all but suffocating condominium. If there was any residual guilt over having figuratively "abandoned" her sister, being there for Sam far outweighed it in her eyes.

Sam needed her, whether the man realized that fact or not.

Celia, she thought, never did.

Chapter 15

Though Johnny Vine's head never moved, his eyes slid around the corners of the interrogation room with the effortless movements of a snake, taking in everything in its path.

Apparently Vine, Sam thought, was not the laid-back man Zoe seemed to indicate he was. Vine might *look* sleepy, but Sam was willing to bet very little got past the man. An obvious bodybuilder, the six-foot Vine wore a dark blue T-shirt that clung and made love to every muscle on his upper torso.

It was difficult to say what Vine was proudest of, his muscles or the gaudy, multicolored tattoo of a hummingbird on his left forearm. Besides his eyes, the tattoo was the only other thing that moved. He was continually flexing his forearm.

Nerves? Sam wondered.

Was this the media's Alphabet Killer, or just some self-centered narcissist in love with his own reflection? Sam caught the man studying himself in the room's one-way mirror.

What had Celia seen in him? Or had she just used Vine, the way she had used everyone else who crossed her path? He had a feeling it was most likely the latter.

Sam sat in the chair opposite his suspect, scrutinizing Vine in silence. He was in here alone with a possible serial killer despite the fact that Zoe had asked to be included in the room when he questioned Celia's ex-boyfriend.

Under the circumstances, the best he could do was to allow her to view the interview, as this procedure was whimsically referred to, through the one-way window. She was a civilian and unless she was Vine's lawyer, she couldn't be in the room when he was conducting the interview.

After the lengthy pause, Sam began with an observation based on the notes written in Vine's file—after some creative digging, one had turned up. Vine's name had been misspelled.

"You seem to live well," Sam observed.

Johnny Vine grinned, turning his tanned, handsome face into something just short of bordering on wicked. "I do okay."

Sam tapped the file on the table between them. "Yet it says here you have no steady source of income. What is it exactly that you do, Mr. Vine?" Sam asked.

The deep blue eyes met his unflinchingly. "I'm an entrepreneur."

It never ceased to amaze Sam how criminals managed to dress up what they actually did in an effort to make it sound legitimate.

"You mean you're a drug dealer," Sam corrected.

"I mean I'm an entrepreneur," Vine repeated, the smug smile on his lips never wavering.

"It says in here," Sam indicated the file with his eyes, "that you were busted and charged with dealing in narcotics."

Johnny leaned back in his chair, tilting on two of the four legs. "It should also say there that the charges were dropped. Besides, that's all ancient history," he told Sam, dismissing the allegations with a condescending wave of his hand. And then his eyes narrowed. "What's this really about?"

Sam didn't bother to preface his statement. He wanted to see Vine's reaction—how good an actor was this man? "Celia Robison was murdered last weekend."

Vine responded as if he'd just been told a news item about someone he hardly knew rather than someone he would have supposedly dragged away in a jealous ragc from her own wedding.

"Yeah. I heard about that. Too bad."

Sam felt his temper surge. For two cents, he would have wrung the man's neck and felt as if he'd done society a service.

But he liked his job and doing something like that would definitely cost him his badge. He was supposed to protect and serve, not mete out justice, no matter how well-deserved he might think it was.

So he reined in his temper and continued the questioning in a deceptively calm voice. "Rumor has it that you did it."

Vine looked completely unfazed by the accusation. "You and I both know rumors are a dime a dozen, Detective. Besides, she was killed— When did you say it was?" he asked, cocking his head as if it would make him hear the answer more clearly.

"I didn't," Sam said pointedly, then answered the man's implied question. "She was killed Saturday morning, between ten and ten fifteen."

Vine made a show of taking in the information. "Narrow window," he commented.

Sam's eyes narrowed as he struggled to curb his loathing. "Too narrow for you to crawl out of."

That was when Vine laughed. "Sorry to disappoint you, man, but I've got an alibi. I was in Vegas last weekend, trying to work up a little business. And you know Vegas. Cameras everywhere. I'm sure if you go through enough footage, you'll find me on it, every minute of that narrow window." He was fairly gloating as he gave the information.

"Which casino?" Sam demanded, his voice low, dangerous. Vine's laugh was getting under his skin in the worst way.

Vine pretended to think over the question. "All of them," he responded flippantly. "Lady Luck doesn't stay put, you know," he added glibly. "Can I go now?" Vine wanted to know. "Seeing as how you've got nothing to hold me on."

"You can go," Sam growled the response. "Just don't leave town."

"I don't plan to, at least not for a while." His reply was fraught with insolence. "By the way, tell Celia's little sister I said hi," he told Sam, nodding toward the mirrored wall. "I figure she's standing back there, seeing as how she's probably the one who told you about me."

Sam's response was immediate. "What's the matter? Don't you think I can do detective work on my own?" he asked Vine with more than a trace of cynicism.

Vine didn't answer yes or no. Instead, he said, "I think you utilize people, same as me, Detective."

With a dismissive nod, Vine rose to his feet. The jeans that clung to his body had seen better days, but his hand-tooled boots were brand new and buffed to a high gloss.

He looked like a faux cowboy in search of a song, Sam thought. To each his own.

One hand on the doorknob, Vine paused to say, "Don't take this the wrong way, Detective, but I hope not to see you again."

"We'll see how this plays out," Sam responded. "I can have someone walk you out," he offered.

The path from here to the front exit was not straightforward. The last thing he wanted was to have Vine wandering around in the halls.

"Don't bother. I know my way around here," Vine assured him.

Which, Sam thought, contradicted the notion that the man had last been charged a long time ago. Someone had covered for Vine, probably in exchange for some free drugs, Sam surmised.

"He's got an alibi?" Zoe came into the room the moment Vine had walked out and crossed the hall. Her distress was right there on her face for everyone to see.

"He *says* he has an alibi," Sam stressed, then pointed out, "Big difference."

Sam was obviously not going to take Vine's word for it, she thought. That left only one path to take as far as she could see.

"Does that mean you're going to send someone to the casinos in Las Vegas to review the videos on their security cameras?" It seemed like a huge project from where she was standing.

He'd thought of that and dismissed it. That approach was far too labor-intensive.

"No, I'm going to have Trevor pull some strings and have Vine's photograph circulated around the casinos to see if anyone remembers seeing him. If any of the employees at a specific casino say yes, *then* I'm going to have Trevor requisition the videos—or have them run at the casino using a facial recognition program."

She grinned at him. Maybe things were coming together after all. "It's good to know people."

"When they're the 'right' people," he corrected pointedly.

Taking out his cell phone, Sam lost no time in getting in contact with his brother.

Trevor picked up after the third ring.

"I need a little interdepartmental cooperation," Sam told the oldest of his siblings.

"What's up?" It was obvious Sam had gotten his attention.

Sam explained the problem to him and succinctly stated what he needed done. He didn't have the kind of authority which allowed him to cross state lines with the investigation. Of course, he could ask for cooperation, but that was such a subjective thing that Sam felt it best to hand this part of the investigation into the murder over to his brother. This was, after all, considered part of a serial killing spree and as such, belonged in the hands of the FBI.

Trevor listened quietly to the narrative, then said, "Send me this suspect's picture and I'll have someone here get started with the search."

"Thanks," Sam said, unable to elaborate his feelings any further than that.

"Hey, what are siblings for?" Trevor responded just before he terminated the connection.

For a while there, after Trevor had turned eighteen, there'd been some resentment among the others that the oldest of their family didn't attempt to get custody of the rest of them, thereby springing them out of the hell that had made up their county's foster care system.

But looking back now, Sam could see what Trevor's

dilemma had been. One eighteen-year-old, without any real visible means of support, suing for custody of six other kids. Trevor would have been laughed right out of the courthouse.

But at the time all he and the others knew was that they had been abandoned—again—this time by their own sibling. It had been a very difficult thing to come to terms with.

"Trevor's on it," Sam told Zoe as he put away his cell phone.

"You don't think Johnny's the Alphabet Killer, do you?" Zoe guessed. Although she didn't want to, she was harboring the same sort of doubts she saw in Sam's eyes.

Sam shook his head as he walked out of the interrogation area with Zoe and back to where his desk was located.

"No, I don't. These women were handpicked because of their looks and their names. In all likelihood, they were probably stalked by the killer. No matter how hard I tried, I couldn't find any connection between them or between each of them and Johnny. But his connection to your sister," he concluded, "is obvious."

"What about the alibi?" she wanted to know, hoping that fell apart. If it did, it would be that much easier to nail Vine.

"Right now, it's just a lot of talk. He probably thought we don't have the manpower to disprove his story and until we do, for all intents and purposes, we have to view it as true."

"But you do have the manpower," she said excitedly. "You have Trevor."

"Fortunately for us," Sam acknowledged with a nod of his head. Reaching his desk, he looked down at the stack of papers that looked in imminent danger of falling over and scattering. "Look, I've got some paperwork to catch up on that has nothing to do with your sister's murder or the serial killer. Why don't you go home and see about catching up on some of your own things?" he suggested. "And I'll get back to you."

She looked at Sam doubtfully, thinking he was just trying to brush her off. She supposed she couldn't really blame him. After all, she represented a momentary lapse in his judgment, a quick fling at best, but now it was time for him to get back to the rest of his life and he was politely sending her back to hers.

Zoe reminded herself that she'd gotten more than she had hoped for. And, okay, she'd hoped it could go on until this murder was wrapped up, but not everything turned out the way a person might hope it would, she reminded herself.

So, silently vowing to put up a good front and not suddenly turn into a clingy woman that would make Sam regret the time they'd had together, she nodded, agreeing with his suggestion.

"Okay, sure," she replied, willing herself to sound upbeat even if it was the last thing she felt. "I'll get out of your way."

"Zoe," he called after her as she started to walk toward the hall.

Part of her wanted to keep on walking, to at least cling to that dignity and exit, head held high. But that might seem petulant.

And besides, she could no more pretend to ignore his voice than she could turn into the swan she longed to be, so she stopped and looked at him over her shoulder, waiting for him to say something more.

"Yes?"

"I *will* get back to you," he repeated, this time with an assurance in his voice that there was no way she could miss.

Zoe believed him.

She smiled then and said, "Okay."

And this time, as she turned and walked away from the office, she didn't feel as if she was walking away from the best moment of her life and back into the sidelines again.

Though he lowered his head as if he was getting back to the work he had mentioned, Sam watched as Zoe left the room. The set of her shoulders told him that she'd believed him.

Sam smiled to himself.

He knew he shouldn't have said anything, that he should have just let her keep walking, in effect out of his life. But he just couldn't bring himself to do it, to let go the way he knew he should because it was best for her. She was too good to be mixed up with the likes of him. Someone like Zoe deserved a man who wasn't haunted by his own set of demons, who actually believed in things like love and happiness.

If he was truly a decent man, he reasoned, he would have let her go.

But while he was striving to do his best to achieve that status, to actually *be* a decent man, Sam found that he needed something to give light to the darkness in his life.

And Zoe was that light.

He wasn't strong enough to let her go. At least, not yet.

The best he could hope for, for her sake, was that she woke up on her own.

In the meantime, he told himself, if he didn't get to this stack of paperwork that just seemed to be multiplying on its own at an alarming rate as it sat there on his desk, he was never going to be able to get out of the police station before the next New Year's Day.

With a sigh, he got started, daring himself to see just how long he would last at this.

Zoe drove to her house humming.

She knew very well that she shouldn't be getting her hopes up, but she couldn't help herself. Sam had told her he'd get back to her. There was no reason for him to say that if he hadn't meant it, so what that told her was, if nothing else, this wonderful interlude in her life—she wasn't foolish enough to think it was something more than that—was going to go on for at least a little while longer.

With any luck, she suddenly thought, Sam might even stop by tonight.

The very thought caused an excitement to take hold of her.

She needed to swing by the market, she thought. In case Sam *did* stop by her place, she wanted to have something special prepared for him and there was almost nothing in her refrigerator. She hadn't felt like eating since the murder.

She had no idea what Sam's preferences were when it came to food, only that, like most Texans, he liked meat. Using that as a basis, she figured beef stew with a slew of vegetables was a safe bet. So that was the first thing she bought, along with a six-pack of beer. If Sam *didn't* come by tonight, the beer would keep indefinitely and the stew could last for several days before it needed to be eaten or thrown away.

Zoe put her plan in motion.

She made her purchases, along with a few extra things, and was on her way home within an hour. She was fairly pleased with herself and looking forward to cooking, something she *always* looked forward to. Cooking, creating something from scratch, relaxed her.

Feeling extra hopeful and energized, she pulled up into her driveway.

She had a penchant for trying to unload her car in one full swoop and today was no different. So, with her arms filled with grocery bags, she made her way to her front door.

Creatively balancing the bags, she unlocked her door, went inside and then pushed the door closed using her back.

Home, she thought with a smile.

It was exactly one second before she actually focused on her surroundings, and one and a half seconds before she saw that her house had been ransacked.

Just like Celia's had.

Chapter 16

Like a woman caught up in a nightmare, grocery bags still pressed against her chest like protective shields, Zoe walked into the center of the living room. She looked around her in utter disbelief.

Only a few hours had passed since she'd been here.

How could all this have happened so fast?

Everything in sight had been upended and either torn apart or thrown aside. Whoever had turned Celia's condo upside down looking for something had taken their search here.

Judging by the absolute blitzkrieg appearances, since *everything* looked as if it had been ransacked, whatever they were looking for, they hadn't found it.

But what was "it"?

What could they possibly think she had here in her house? Did they think Celia had hidden something here to keep it out of their hands?

Zoe couldn't begin to sort any of this out. The first

step to recreating order and getting to the bottom of all this was to call Sam. Sam might be able to tell her something if she pressed him about it.

She knew that as a rule, Sam didn't volunteer things readily, but this wasn't some casual exchange she wanted to have with him, wheedling information out of him to satisfy some sort of curious bent she had. This was serious.

Very serious, she thought, looking around again.

It was then that Zoe realized she was still holding on to the bags of groceries she'd brought into the house, holding on to them as if they could somehow provide her with a buffer against whatever it was that was going on here. She needed to put them down somewherc, out of the way.

When she turned to put the grocery bags down on the sofa, that was when she suddenly became aware of it.

Aware of the feel of cold metal pressed against her temple.

Aware of the low, growling voice that angrily demanded, "Where is it? Where's the key?"

Doing her damnedest not to tremble, she took a step back to find herself looking down the muzzle of a midsize handgun.

The person holding the gun and issuing the demanding question was the same person she'd seen in the precinct more than an hour ago.

Johnny Vine.

Vine, looking a way she had never seen him look

before. Not the laid-back, devil-may-care rootless boyfriend, but someone who was desperate.

"I'm not going to ask you twice," he warned, his eyes cold, flat. Dangerous.

"What key?" Zoe cried. "What are you talking about? I don't have any key that belongs to you."

"It's not the *key* that belongs to me," Vine retorted, succeeding in making the whole issue even more unclear to her than it already was. "Now *where the hell is it*?" He cocked the gun, his meaning crystal clear. She either produced the key he was looking for, or she forfeited her life.

Desperate, Zoe took the only chance she had. She shoved the grocery bags in her arms at him with all of her might.

Curses littered the air. The gun discharged but she was already running when it did.

Because she was so shaken, Zoe reacted automatically and, still running, looked down at her torso to see if she was bleeding anywhere. Her adrenaline was ramped up so high, she doubted if she would have been able to feel the bullet if it *had* struck her. Not until she made good her getaway, at any rate.

But she saw no blood. The bullet had apparently missed her.

Relieved, more frightened than she'd ever been in her entire life, Zoe flew out of her house.

Hitting the driveway, she just kept on running. She wasn't going to even attempt to get into her car—which was right there—because she knew Vine would be on her before she ever got a chance to put the key in the ignition, much less start the engine and peel out of there.

She might be faster than he was, but he was a great deal stronger. Her best chance to get away was to run. She'd been on the track team, both in high school and in college, and she'd never gotten out of the habit of running. Running was her way of relieving her stress. Some people drank, she ran.

And she was never more grateful for keeping up that form of exercise than she was right at this moment, despite the fact that she was now covering ground in four-inch heels.

No longer encumbered by grocery bags, Zoe'd flown out of her house like the proverbial bat out of hell. She continued going and ran out of her cul-de-sac and down a through street in her development, all the while trying to think of whose door to knock on in order to get someone to dial 911.

She was still trying to decide, continually looking over her shoulder to make sure Johnny Vine wasn't pursuing her, when the sudden screech of tires registered. From the sound, it seemed as if a car was making a sudden, unexpected U-turn in the middle of the street.

Afraid Vine was now pursuing her in his car, she spun around and began to run in an alternate direction. The man whose eyes she'd looked into in her living room was desperate and would think nothing of running her down if she didn't volunteer the location of a key she knew nothing about.

Her lungs were bursting now as she poured it on.

The car with the screeching tires was still coming after her, she could tell by the noise that was growing louder.

And then, just like that, the car was cutting off her avenue of escape, pinning her in such a fashion that there was nowhere for her to go.

Her heart pounding wildly in her throat, Zoe searched for anything she could use as a weapon. Seeing a garden gnome on the front of a lawn, she lunged for it. She held it up like a weapon as the driver emerged from behind the wheel.

The gnome slid from her fingers onto the grass as her knees threatened to buckle right out from under her.

"Sam!" she all but sobbed as she threw her arms around him. "Thank God it's you! But that's not your car," she cried in confusion. She wouldn't have kept on running like that if she'd known it was he.

He'd had to switch cars at the station. When he came out, he'd found his battery had inexplicably gone dead despite the fact that it was only a year old. An equally inexplicable sense of urgency had him switching cars rather than waiting to see if his battery had indeed given up the ghost, or simply needed to be jumped.

Seeing Zoe running down the street, he knew he was right to hurry back to her.

"What the hell is going on?" he wanted to know, holding her to him. "You're shaking like a leaf."

Now that Sam was here to protect her, she had to struggle to keep herself from falling apart. It took her a minute to catch her breath. "Johnny—Johnny was in my house."

He knew it. He knew he should have found some reason to keep Vine locked up until he could conduct a further investigation into the man's dealings. He could have kicked himself for letting the man loose.

Drawing Zoe back so he could look at her, he searched her face for telltale marks. "Did Vine do something to you?"

She sucked in some more air and began to breathe a little more evenly.

"He ransacked my house, just like he did Celia's. I must have walked in on him. He was looking for some key," she told Sam. "Demanded to know where it was." Her mouth went dry as she went on to say, "He had a gun."

The look on Sam's face went from compassionate to stone-cold. "Get in the car," he ordered.

She did, although by the look on her face, it appeared that she was operating on automatic pilot.

He would have had her stay in his car and lock the doors while he went back to her place on foot, but he could get to her house faster with the car than if he ran, the way she had.

Driving like a man possessed, he got to Zoe's house within two minutes.

"Stay in the car," Sam ordered. "And call for backup."

Getting out of the vehicle, he tossed his cell phone on the seat next to her. It was easier that way. He didn't have time to instruct her on how to use the radio in the car to call the station.

His weapon drawn and the safety off, Sam approached her house.

The door was standing wide open, just the way he assumed she'd left it when she'd flown out of the house. Sam entered, scanning the area as he inched his way into first the living room, then the kitchen and the family room beyond that. Because he had no backup, progress was torturously slow.

He proceeded the same way throughout the whole first floor, taking care not to step or trip on anything. It was far from easy. Vine had done as thorough a job here as he had done in Celia's condo, Sam thought.

What was this key he was trying to find? And more importantly, what did it open?

Weapon raised above shoulder level, Sam made his way up the stairs, then went through the bedrooms one at a time, alert for any noise, any sudden movements.

Only when he had satisfied himself that he had cleared the entire floor did he allow himself to relax a little.

Until he heard something coming from the first floor. Instantly alert again, Sam made his way quickly to the stairs, then down them, scanning the area relentlessly until it almost hurt his eyes to do so.

When he saw the shadow cast by a figure in the living room, he came perilously close to shooting—until he saw the shadow belonged to Zoe.

Furious over what had almost happened, he angrily snapped, "I thought I told you to stay in the damn car," as he came down the last couple of steps.

She didn't back down in the face of his anger. "You were taking so long, I was afraid something had happened to you. I wanted to help."

"And you coming in and getting shot would have helped?" he demanded.

The moment the words were out of his mouth, he regretted them. She was worried about him—when was the last time someone had actually expressed those sentiments? He'd been on his own and independent for so long, he couldn't begin to remember the last time he'd felt someone cared about him.

"Vine's gone," he told her, abruptly changing subjects and his tone. "Do you have any idea what key he could have been referring to?"

She shook her head. "Celia never said anything about a key, or about holding something for Johnny. That's what this has got to be about, right? She had something of his and then locked it up, I guess. Either for safekeeping—or as an insurance policy to keep him from doing something to her."

Yeah, and look how well that turned out for her,

Sam thought, but he kept it to himself. As for Zoe's theory, it was plausible enough, he supposed.

"Yeah, but what? And where?" He sighed as he heard the sound of approaching sirens. "One thing's clear, though."

She looked at him, waiting for him to elaborate. When he didn't, she prodded, "What?"

"You can't stay here. It's not safe."

She hated this. Hated the fact that Vine had made her afraid to stay in her own house. And Sam was right. She couldn't stay here, at least not right now. Not while all of this was still up in the air and Celia's killer was still out there. "I can get a hotel room for a few days," she agreed. By then, her nerves should have settled down. "But after that—"

"No hotel room," he told her, vetoing the idea with finality, leaving absolutely no room for argument. "You're staying with me. That way I can keep an eye on you around the clock. And when I can't, I'll have a guard posted nearby."

Not that the idea of having him so close didn't sound lovely to her, but it also made her feel guilty. "You have work to do. You can't waste your time being my bodyguard."

"I don't consider that a waste of my time. Arguing with you about it, though, *is* a waste of my time," he pointed out. "Go pack whatever you need to take with you—and leave any useless protests about it behind here," he instructed.

If she did have the notion to carry on any further

discussion with him about it, it had to be tabled because the next minute, the house began to fill up with police personnel connected to the Granite Gulch PD's forensics team.

The head of the team, a twenty-three-year veteran of the force named Lieutenant Gary Reynolds, looked around at the destruction and debris that littered the small living room.

He shook his head. Even for chaotic, this set a new high. "I see this is another fine mess you've gotten us into," the older man quipped.

"I don't make the messes, I just call in about them," Sam told the lieutenant, holding up his hands as if he was literally surrendering as he protested his innocence. "And while you're doing your 'thing,' Lieutenant," he said, making a request of the other man, "see if you can come across a key."

"A key?" Reynolds repeated uncertainly. "What kind of key?"

"Damned if I know," Sam admitted, then hazarded a guess. "Like one for a gym locker or maybe a storage unit. Something maybe out of the ordinary, I'm thinking," Sam elaborated for the crime scene investigator. "Better yet, bag and tag any keys you find and then have them sent to me."

While he was talking to the lieutenant, out of the corner of his eye he saw Zoe suddenly look very alert, as if she'd just had an unexpected thought.

Had she remembered something?

Had his innocuous instructions to the head of the

crime scene investigation triggered something in her memory? He could only hope.

Finished with Reynolds, Sam took Zoe aside. “You remember something?” he asked her gently.

“Maybe,” she qualified warily.

She didn’t want Sam to get his hopes up if she turned out to be wrong. And who knew, maybe she’d only imagined it. Maybe she was trying so hard to remember, to connect the dots, she was actually creating something in her mind that had never happened.

Sam struggled to curb his impatience.

“Now’s not the time to be coy, Zoe. Now’s the time to jump in, both feet first. As much as I like the idea of guarding that body of yours, both of us will breathe a lot easier once Vine is off the streets and behind bars where that piece of filth belongs.”

“You’re probably right,” Zoe agreed. The more she knew about Johnny Vine, the more convinced she was that he was the type of person whose own mother wouldn’t vouch for him. “But there’s still nothing to tie him to the other two murders. And if there’s no connection, then he’s probably not the Alphabet Killer.”

Sam wasn’t finished conducting his investigation into that and until it was completed, he reserved judgment on whether or not to absolve Vine of the annoying nickname the media had given him.

“We’ll weigh the evidence on that when the time comes. Right now, I’ve got him for attacking you.” He took her chin in his hand and examined her face again, more closely this time. First one side, then the other.

Zoe stifled her urge to pull her face away. Instead, she waited for Sam to finish examining it. "What are you doing?" she wanted to know.

"Making sure there are no bruises," Sam told her.

"Johnny didn't attack me physically," she told Sam, thinking they had already established that fact when she'd initially told him what had happened. "He just pointed his gun at me." And then she remembered something she hadn't mentioned to him. "They'll probably find a bullet embedded in something."

"He *shot* at you?" Sam asked, hardly able to contain his fury.

She nodded. "In a way. The gun went off when I threw the groceries at him."

"Hold it. Back up," he told her, holding up one hand like a traffic cop. "*What* groceries?"

She didn't think that was really important in the scheme of things, but since he'd asked, she elaborated. "I stopped at the store to pick up a few things—I thought maybe you'd come by after work and I knew you'd be hungry. I didn't have anything decent in my refrigerator—just some leftover takeout that's probably turning if it hasn't already turned by now. Anyway, I picked up a few things."

He considered what she'd just told him. *No one* had ever put that much thought into his care and feeding. He could remember going hungry for more than a couple of days because of one thing or another during his days in foster care.

And he could have lost her so easily just now. Lost her to a criminal's bullet before he ever even had a chance to bring her into his life for more than a day at a time. All Vine had to do was shoot before she had a chance to throw anything at him to deflect the shot and she could have been dead.

The very thought numbed him.

"I guess it was lucky you were carrying groceries, then," was his only comment. He didn't trust himself to say anything further right now.

He needed time to process the rest of it. But for now, there was still one question he hadn't gotten the answer to. "What was it you just remembered?" he pressed.

Getting caught up with Sam, she'd almost forgotten again. But his question brought it all vividly back to her.

"Celia had a storage unit she rented," she told him, adding hopefully, "Maybe that's the key that Johnny is so desperately searching for."

Chapter 17

Had Zoe's house not been filled with crime scene investigators milling around in every conceivable room, he would have kissed her. Remembering Celia had recently rented a storage unit might just give them the break in the case they needed—or at least he fervently hoped so.

Hell, the way he felt right now, he would have kissed Zoe if she'd just recited the alphabet and missed mentioning some of the key vowels.

For his own peace of mind, Sam chalked up his reaction, as well as his feelings for Zoe in general, as being the way they were because this was all new to him, this feeling of lightness and hope that she inspired within him. New and different and after living in the darkness every day for so long, this was an incredible and more than welcome change.

But he couldn't fool himself, Sam silently warned. He couldn't allow himself to make more of it than it really was. To do so went against his nature, against everything he was and had ever been. Some people saw rainbows after a storm. He saw only a temporary break between two storms.

Shaking off any philosophical bent, Sam forced himself to focus on the immediate problem: the case, not the internal tug-of-war he currently was unsuccessfully waging.

"Great, now all we need to do is figure out where she rented her unit." That meant it was time for some good old-fashioned police work. The kind that required shoe leather, patience and a lot of questioning.

"She's had the storage unit for about three months," Zoe recalled. "Wouldn't there be some kind of billing statement from the facility?" she questioned enthusiastically. It seemed only logical to her.

But Sam was more guarded about his reaction. "She might have paid for the unit when she opened it, then given them the rent for six months, or maybe a year—cash, up-front," he emphasized. "If she did that, there would be no paper trail."

Zoe looked at him, surprised he would say something like that. "You didn't know Celia very well at all, did you?"

"Why?" he asked sharply. He didn't see where one thing had anything to do with the other.

"Because if you did," Zoe answered him patiently, "you'd know she never paid cash for anything. She wanted to sustain an illusion for herself that money was going to last her for all eternity."

She'd lost count of the number of times that Celia had "borrowed" money from her and then conveniently forgotten to repay it.

"Celia paid *everything* with either checks or credit cards. She maxed out at least two of them, if not more, but what that means is that there had to be a statement from the storage facility somewhere and once we find it, we have the name of the place—not to mention the unit number and all that good stuff."

She stopped talking because she realized Sam was just staring at her. Feeling self-conscious, she asked him, "Something wrong?"

"Not a thing," he answered a bit too quickly.

This wasn't a discussion he wanted to get into, but what he was actually doing was trying to find Zoe's flaws. Everyone had them. Some had a lot more than their share. But so far, though, the more he knew about Zoe, the more flawless she seemed to become. She was intelligent, sweet, selfless, kind—the list just went on. It didn't seem possible that a person of her caliber actually existed, and yet…

Get it together, Colton. You're looking for a serial killer and trying to find clues to the last known whereabouts of your mother's remains. You don't have time for this other stuff.

"Wait right here. Let me just tell Reynolds to have his people on the lookout for a billing statement belonging to a storage facility, and then we can get out of here," Sam told her.

* * *

When he returned to the living room a few minutes later, he found Zoe on the floor, gathering up the various items that had been packed in the grocery bags she'd shoved at Vine. The bags themselves were no longer of any use, having ripped apart as they first hit their target, then the floor.

Crossing to her, he asked Zoe, "What are you doing?"

Zoe didn't bother to look up. She was hurrying as fast as she could, stashing things in a large canvas bag she kept in her hall closet.

"Picking up dinner," she answered glibly.

"I think that's called tampering with evidence," he corrected.

"I threw the bags at Johnny. No big mystery there, nothing to examine or deduce. You won't find any clues here—I certainly didn't manage to even render him unconscious, because if I had, you would have found him on the floor when you came back instead of just the groceries."

He laughed. "You know, you'd make a pretty sharp little lawyer. Let me go back and clear this with Reynolds for formality's sake, although I don't see him saying no," he told her. "But just for the time being, leave all that where it is."

She rose to her feet the way he told her to and left everything alone. She wanted this to be over with as soon as possible.

Sam returned in less than three minutes with the

lieutenant right behind him. Rather than saying anything, Reynolds raised the camera that was part of his equipment and at times, practically part of him, as well. He took several shots of the groceries on the floor to preserve the scene, then waved Zoe on.

"You're free to take the groceries with you," he told her.

He didn't have to say it twice.

"Wow. I had no idea you could cook this well. Hell, I had no idea *anyone* could cook this well," Sam confessed, feeling as if he might have overeaten.

Getting up from the table, Zoe began to clear it. "Like I said before, librarians do a lot of reading." She stacked their plates together, putting the utensils on top. "You'd be surprised how many cookbooks wind up being donated to the used bookstore attached to the library," she told him.

Sam looked at her, puzzled by the used bookstore reference.

"Not something I'd be aware of," he admitted. "Last time I remember being in the public library I was a freshman in high school, and the only reason I was there in the first place was because I didn't want to go to the place that was my current 'home' at the time."

Zoe stopped gathering dishes for a moment. "Why not?"

"I was fifteen and Mrs. Foster Parent kept hitting on me whenever we were alone. Her husband was this big, hulking guy and I think you get the picture." Too many people, he quickly learned from firsthand experience, were part of the foster parent system strictly for the money.

Moved, Zoe touched his face. It hurt her to think of him in that sort of a situation. She'd known him back then, or at least had been very aware of him. But she'd never had a clue what he was going through at the time.

"I used to feel sorry for myself because I was such a wallflower. I'll take being sheltered and neglected over what you must have gone through every time," she told him quietly.

Sam took her hands in his and pulled her down onto his lap.

The dishes and everything else were forgotten about for the time being as they sought comfort in each other's arms.

The next morning, Sam lost no time tracking down the name of the storage company that Celia had used. Since he hadn't heard from Reynolds, he assumed no one had found the billing statement he'd asked about. The next course of action was to access Celia's checking account. Once he had the list of checks she'd written in the last month, it wasn't difficult finding one written to a storage facility.

The facility was located just on the outskirts of Granite Gulch.

The person who ran the front office was out when he and Zoe arrived at the storage facility.

"We could wait," Zoe suggested, nodding at the Out to Lunch sign hanging in the dusty window.

Rather than answer her, Sam doubled back to his car, popped the trunk and took out the bull cutters he kept there.

"Or not," Zoe concluded as she followed Sam onto the grounds and ultimately, to the storage unit they had discovered, via a further review of her cancelled checks, belonged to Celia.

One quick movement of Sam's wrists and the lock, rendered useless, fell to the ground.

The surge of triumph over finding the unit and gaining access quickly turned to disappointment when they went inside. Aside from holding what appeared to be every article of clothing Celia had ever owned, there wasn't very much stored in the unit.

The handful of boxes that were piled up in one of the corners contained various memorabilia that obviously meant something to Celia, but not to the average person looking through them.

None of the boxes contained a key. A quick, more thorough search of the small area neglected to produce the key that seemed to mean so much to Vine.

"Another wild goose chase," Sam muttered in disgust, momentarily stumped as to their next course of action.

Just then, his cell phone began to pulse, demanding immediate attention. There were times when he hated that sound, Sam thought.

"Colton," he answered half a beat after he'd pulled the phone out of his pocket.

Zoe listened to his side of the conversation and watched his face, trying to read between the lines. The lines she discerned were dark and foreboding.

"Got it," she heard him conclude grimly. "I've got something to do first, but I'll be there as soon as I'm finished."

With that, he terminated the call and put the phone back into his pocket.

"What do you have to do first?" she asked, an uneasy feeling undulating through her stomach. *And where are you going after that?*

"Drop you off at my place." Sam took hold of her arm, ushering her out of the storage unit.

Being around Sam these past few days had made her bolder. The old Zoe would have never asked, "Why can't I come with you?" But Sam's lover could, and did.

Sam pulled down the unit's retractable door and walked with her to his car. Passing the front office, he noticed the manager hadn't returned yet.

"Because there's been another murder," he told Zoe, "and I think you've seen enough dead people to last you a lifetime. I'm not taking you to another grisly crime scene." Sam's tone made it clear there was no room for argument.

Even so, she had to try just once. "I could be useful to you. I might see something you don't."

Sam shot her down crisply. "That's CSI's job," he informed her. They got into the vehicle. "I'll be back as soon as I can," he promised.

She knew what that meant. Any time between ninety minutes and thirty-six hours—or more. But there was nothing she could do about it so she merely made the best of the situation and nodded.

"Her name's Daphne Picard," the first officer on the scene told him thirty minutes later.

Sam had just left Zoe in the care of one of the uniformed officers he worked with on a regular basis, instructing the man to be on the lookout for Vine.

All the way over to the house in Rosewood, a town neighboring Granite Gulch, he tried to shake the uneasy feeling that something was wrong.

He told himself what he was focusing on was this murder, which by definition was the "something wrong" since murder was such an unnatural act.

But it felt like something more than that.

The job was getting him paranoid, Sam thought, especially now that there was actually someone whom, whether he liked it or not, he cared about a great deal.

Sam found it was taking more and more of an effort to ignore that simple fact. It kept breaking through his consciousness at the most inopportune times.

Forcing himself to focus exclusively on the details

of this latest murder, he took the pertinent information in quickly.

Daphne Picard was a single woman in her early twenties. Like the others, she had long brown hair and, also like the others, she'd been shot and the killer had painted a bull's-eye on her forehead with an asymmetric red dot in the bull's-eye, just off to the left.

The crazy SOB's still at it, he thought grimly.

And, according to the medical examiner's preliminary approximate time of death, Vine couldn't have done it. He'd been in custody at the time.

Back to square one.

Sam remained just long enough to review the crime scene and make a few notes to himself. Conferring with the first officer on the scene, he asked to be sent any and all reports the crime generated.

Finished for the time being, Sam went outside and placed a call to Zoe. He had a sudden need just to hear her voice.

His call went to voice mail.

Twice.

Telling himself there were half a dozen reasons why his call hadn't gotten through to her, he put in a call to the officer he'd left guarding his house.

There was no answer there, either.

At this point, Sam didn't even bother trying to speculate what was going on and why neither Zoe nor the officer was answering their phones. He needed to know the actual reason why they weren't.

After hurrying to his car, he jumped in and didn't even remember starting it up.

The only thing he was aware of was that he had to get there.

Now.

The police officer's car was just where Sam remembered having seen it: parked at the curb directly in front of his house. The officer, Allen Davidson, was sitting behind the steering wheel.

So why the hell wasn't he answering his cell phone?

Sam pulled up beside the police vehicle, several rather choice words hot on his tongue.

He never got a chance to utter any of them.

The officer wasn't sitting up in the driver's seat. He was slumped over in it, a fresh bullet hole in his temple.

Cursing himself for leaving Zoe, Sam left his car double-parked beside the dead officer's vehicle as he raced to his front door.

It was closed, but Sam quickly discovered it wasn't locked.

He pulled his weapon out as he eased the door open all the way and entered his home.

What he really wanted to do was run through the rooms, calling her name, but he knew if she actually still *was* on the premises, all that would do would alert Vine, who, the sick feeling in the pit of his stomach told him, was behind all this.

So although it pained Sam to do so, he slowly made his way through his house, sweeping carefully and efficiently from room to room, on guard to the ever-present possibility that the presumably newly minted cop killer could get the drop on him at any moment.

The painful crawl went on until Sam finally cleared the last room.

A sense of vast disappointment mingled with a tinge of relief within him, the latter born of the fact that Vine wasn't there to get the drop on him. The disappointment came from the same source.

If Vine wasn't here, where was he?

And much more importantly, where was Zoe?

For the first time in recent years, Sam stood all but frozen in place, his next move completely and frustratingly eluding him.

When the phone in his pocket vibrated, he jumped as if he'd been poked with a cattle prod. Pulling it out of his pocket, Sam almost dropped the cell before he had the chance to hit the green square, allowing him to accept the call.

"Colton!" he barked into the phone.

"I got something of yours, Colton," the voice on the other end of the call said with a sneering air of superiority. "But, lucky for you, I'm willing to make a trade." There was a long, dramatic pause. Vine, Sam thought, was loving this. He fisted his free hand at his side, struggling with his temper as he heard Vine ask, "Are you interested?"

"What do you want?" Sam snapped.

"Right to the point. I like that. You know what I want, Colton," Sam heard Vine say.

Though it killed him to do so, Sam waited, knowing the longer he took to answer, the more off-balance Vine would become.

And he was right.

When he made no immediate response, Vine angrily filled in the blank for him. "The *key*. I want the freaking locker key!" Sam heard him take a breath, as if trying to calm himself. When Vine spoke again, he sounded a little more in control. "You give me the key, and you get her back in one piece. Otherwise, I get to try out all these nifty new tools I've got. You get my drift?" he asked with a blood-chilling laugh.

Chapter 18

A sizzling white rage seized Sam, all but cutting off his air and temporarily interfering with his ability to form words.

Getting the rage under control, Sam issued a warning to what he considered to be the loathsome piece of garbage on the other end of the line.

"You hurt her, you even *touch* a single hair on her head, and there won't be a rock you can hide under, or a corner of the world you can run to where I won't find you. And when I'm done with you, nobody'll ever be able to identify the pieces."

"Well, well, well, the apple doesn't fall far from the tree after all, does it?" he heard Vine laugh. "Don't worry, Dee-tec-tive," Vine deliberately drew his title out, "you do your part and you can have her back just the way you left her."

And then Vine's voice hardened. "And if you don't get me the key, then whatever happens to her is on your head, not mine. You've got three hours," he snarled, then, as if they were having a friendly conversation, Vine said pleasantly, "I'll leave you to your work now."

"Wait a minute," Sam cried, trying to make him remain on the line. "Let me talk to her. How do I know she's even alive?" he demanded.

He heard the same bone-chilling laugh on the other end of the line. "Leap of faith, brother. You've gotta have a leap of faith."

"You expect me to—"

But the phone had already gone dead. Vine had hung up on him.

Sam curbed the sudden, almost overwhelming desire to throw his cell phone against the wall. He knew if he broke his phone, he'd have to waste precious time getting a new one and the insane man he'd just been talking to could call back in the interim. There was no telling what Vine was capable of doing if he didn't get hold of him when he called, Sam thought.

Frustrated, Sam started to curse, then abruptly stopped. There was no point in wasting his breath. He had work to do.

Where the hell was this damn key Vine was going on about?

Searches had been conducted in both Celia's condo and Zoe's house by the forensics team and no one had uncovered an unaccounted-for key in either location. He had personally gone through the storage unit with the same results. There was no key to a locker, or any key at all to be found.

But Vine seemed convinced there was a key, so for now, he was going to work with the assumption that there actually *was* a key.

He got back on his phone and called Reynolds to tell him about the cop who had been killed. With a minimum of words, he explained what was currently going on, asking the head of the crime scene investigative division to go over both residences again, this time with a fine-tooth comb if need be.

Reynolds listened patiently, then said in a voice that never seemed to reflect any sort of agitation, "I don't know if you've heard, but another victim turned up today in Rosewood. Same MO. I'm on my way there with my team."

Sam knew the unit did double duty for both Granite Gulch and Rosewood since the latter town couldn't afford to support a unit its own.

"Yeah, I heard." Sam made his pitch, trying his best not to sound as desperate as he was beginning to feel. "But the girl in Rosewood is already dead. This involves someone who's still alive. But if that key isn't found, then she won't be alive for long."

He heard Reynolds sigh. "Okay. I'll see who I can spare."

"I owe you, Lieutenant," Sam told him.

"Yeah," he heard the man reply in a totally unsympathetic voice, "you do."

* * *

Like a man possessed, Sam drove back to Celia's storage unit.

An hour later, he had gone through everything, searching all four corners of the small unit, taking apart and moving the metal shelves she had put up herself from one side to the other, emptying out all the boxes and putting everything back, one item at a time in case he had missed the key the first time around.

He'd even gone through all the clothing Celia had hung up on the expandable, moveable rods, going through the pockets and then checking the hems to make sure nothing had been sewn into the linings.

The handful of books he found on the shelves had been leafed through systematically, all with the same results. No key.

"Damn it, where the hell is it?" Sam cried, taking a swing at the mobile clothes rack. His punch landed squarely on the metal rod that was holding part of the rack together.

Just like that, the whole rack toppled over on its side.

This time Sam did swear roundly. Disgusted, he was about to leave the rack exactly where it had fallen and just walk out of the unit.

But his overly developed sense of order relentlessly drummed into him as a child had him reconsidering his position.

After a minute he sighed and squatted down beside the rack, looking for the best way to get it upright again while losing a minimum of the hangers that were on the rack. Hangers with clothing.

He struggled with the unwieldy silver rod. That was when he noticed there were uneven cracks in the old wooden floor.

Staring, he could have sworn he saw something catch the light and flash.

It could have very well been his overactive imagination, which, since he'd had little to no sleep of late, had gone into hyperdrive.

Still, he knew he'd have no peace until he checked out the source of the flash, even though, in all likelihood, it was probably a piece of glass that had gotten stuck under the floorboard.

Availing himself of the small, flat penlight he carried, Sam turned it on and shone it slowly along the crack. Just as he was about to stop, something flashed briefly.

He did it again, this time even more slowly. He had the same results.

A third pass allowed him to pinpoint exactly where the flash was coming from.

A quick, impatient search of the unit turned up nothing he could use in order to pry back the wooden board. Sam fell back on the tried and true. He hurried back to his car and got a crowbar out of the trunk.

A nerve-racking five minutes later, he had broken apart the wooden board and found himself staring down at a key.

Hopefully *the* key, not even wanting to entertain the thought that it wasn't.

He had no idea if Celia had hidden the key under the floorboard or if it had just accidentally fallen there—or even if it was the right key. None of that really mattered right now. All that mattered was Vine *believed* it was the key he was looking for.

Without that, Sam knew he didn't have a prayer of getting Zoe back alive.

Vine had given him three hours to come up with the key. He had no way of getting in contact with the man if he found it earlier. The number Vine had used came in as blocked and he had no way to trace it back to its source, which was undoubtedly a burner phone.

He had no choice but to wait for a call back.

Waiting for Vine to call him frayed every single one of Sam's nerves. He spent part of the time trying to be productive by setting up a sting to catch Vine once the man called back with his instructions for the exchange.

When his phone finally did ring, Sam almost jumped out of his skin. Taking a breath, he opened his phone and answered the call.

Vine didn't waste any time. "You have the key?"

"Yes," Sam bit off.

Vine's response was patronizing. "Good man. Knew all you needed was the right motivation."

It took everything Sam had not to tell Vine what he thought of him, or what he would have given anything to *do* to him. Instead, he dutifully played the game. Zoe's life depended on it.

"Where do you want to make the exchange?"

"You know that old abandoned toy warehouse five miles beyond the airport?"

"Yeah, I know it," Sam acknowledged.

"Bring the key there at midnight."

"What about Zoe?" Sam demanded.

Vine's tone was by turns first mocking, then innocent. "What about her?"

Lord, he wanted to pummel the man to the ground. "Let me talk to her."

"Now, don't get pushy," Vine chided as if he were disciplining an eight-year-old. "You'll have plenty of time to talk to her once I have the key."

"Now you listen to me," Sam told him angrily. "I'm not bringing anything anywhere until I get to talk to her."

"You Coltons always were a brash, pushy lot." The laugh was nasty and so chilling, it scraped against the bone.

But a moment later, Sam heard, "Sam?"

Zoe!

Adrenaline shot through him and he held his phone with both hands, afraid he'd drop it. "Zoe. Are you all right? Did he hurt you?"

"Not yet." It was Vine's voice answering his question. He had gotten on the phone again.

"Put her back on!" Sam demanded.

"Don't get greedy, Colton," Vine warned in the

same singsong voice he'd used earlier. "You've got your proof. She's still alive. You want to keep her that way? Bring the key at midnight. See you then."

The line went dead.

The next seven hours dragged by at an incredibly slow pace. Sam had to struggle to keep his impatience from making him implode. He had to hold it together for Zoe's sake, he told himself over and over again.

Although he wanted to be able to capture Vine, his main concern was making sure he got Zoe back alive. He didn't want to risk her life in case the sting went wrong, so while he had a handful of officers strategically planted out of sight around the perimeter of the warehouse, his primary focus at all times was to get Zoe back alive and unharmed.

After her safety was no longer a factor, *then* he could turn his attention to capturing Vine.

Midnight came—and went.

As did twelve fifteen.

Finally, at twelve thirty, Vine stepped out of the shadows of a far corner of the warehouse, seemingly materializing out of nowhere. He had one arm tightly around Zoe's throat while he held a gun to her temple with the other.

The criminal had a flair for drama.

"We're here," Vine announced. "Fashionably late, but here and mostly in one piece."

What the hell was that supposed to mean? "If you hurt her—" Sam began again.

"What? The deal's off?" Vine mocked. "Don't make me laugh. You'll take her any way you can get her and we both know that. But don't worry, she's alive and breathing, although maybe just a little worse for wear for what you and her sister put me through," he tagged on maliciously. "The key?" he demanded sharply, dropping all pretense of friendliness.

Sam took it out of his pocket and held it up. "Come and get it."

"You expect me to walk up to you?" Vine demanded. "How stupid do you think I am?" And then he nodded toward something that was on the floor near where Sam was standing. "See that little yellow toy truck over in the corner? Put the key in the back of truck, point it toward us and turn the switch on. When I get the truck, you get her."

Sam had crossed over to the yellow toy truck, but he made no effort to carry out the rest of Vine's instructions.

"How do I know you'll keep your word?"

"Oh, Sam, you wound me. Have I ever lied to you?" Vine asked mockingly. "Tell you what, I'll let her go when the truck's *almost* here. How's that? Best offer, Sam. Sixty seconds and it's off the table—and she's off her feet," he said nastily, then added, "Permanently."

Sam knew he had no other recourse open to him. His weapon was holstered at his spine. He could definitely access it, but by the time he could aim it, Vine would have pulled the trigger of the gun he was holding against Zoe's temple.

There was only one way to play this.

"We'll do it your way," Sam said through gritted teeth.

"Knew you'd see reason," Vine gloated. "Okay, put the key into the truck." Watching him, Vine waited until his instructions were complied with. "Atta boy, Colton. Now, turn the switch on and aim the truck this way." As he spoke, he raised his elbow, as if poised to pull the gun's trigger if, for some reason, there was so much as a hair's breadth deviation from the truck's path.

Sam did as he was told, depositing the key onto the little truck's flatbed, then releasing the switch. The truck made its way across the warehouse floor.

"The truck's almost there," Sam pointed out a minute later. "Let her go, Vine!"

"Or what, you'll shoot?" Vine mocked. "Don't get your shorts all in a twist, Colton," he laughed. "I'm a man of my word." Vine withdrew his chokehold from around her neck. "Go ahead, sweetheart, he's waiting for you."

As Vine released her, he also pushed Zoe forward, hard, causing her to stumble and fall down from the force of the shove.

Sam ran to her as Vine scooped up the key and ran in the opposite direction, going behind a framework of bare metal shelves.

"I'm fine, go get him," Zoe cried, waving Sam on after the other man.

"Move in, move in," Sam ordered over the shortwave radio he'd had tucked into his back pocket and was now in his hand.

Within seconds, officers descended on the warehouse from all points of outer entry.

Sam ran behind the shelves, toward the area Vine had ducked into.

There was no one there.

A quick search in several directions turned up nothing. Vine had done the impossible. He had vanished from a warehouse surrounded by police officers.

"Where is he?" Zoe cried incredulously, coming up behind him.

"Damned if I know," he bit off in disgust. And then it hit him. "There's got to be some kind of a trap door or an underground tunnel around here, leading away from the warehouse." There was no other explanation. Vine wasn't Houdini.

"Here, Detective," one of the police officers called to Sam.

When Sam turned in that direction, he saw the officer standing before what appeared to be a utility closet. When he drew closer to the closet, Sam saw there was a trapdoor in the floor.

To make his point, the officer indicated the opened trapdoor. "He made his getaway from here," the man told him.

"Find out where that goes," Sam ordered, even though he knew it was probably an exercise in futility.

It was beginning to be clear that Vine was not as dumb as everyone thought. The psychopath had obviously mapped out his getaway long before he placed the ransom call to get his hands on the key that Celia had withheld from him.

"I'm sorry, Sam," Zoe told him as the officers went to follow his orders.

"It's not your fault," he told her. Hooking one arm around her, Sam hugged her to him. "We'll get him," he promised her. "Don't worry about anything, we'll get him." He kissed the top of her head, grateful beyond words she was beside him and all right. "Besides, he hasn't won yet."

It certainly looked that way to Zoe. "But he's got the key."

"Yeah, but I still have an ace in the hole," Sam told her. Looking at the officer closest to him, Sam said, "Plan B, McKinley."

"Yes, sir," the officer said, then turned to the rest of the officers who had rushed into the warehouse in an attempt to capture Vine. "You heard the detective. Plan B."

Zoe looked at Sam, clearly puzzled. "Plan B?" she asked. "There's a plan B?"

He smiled at her, relief still coursing through his veins. He knew it was going to feel like that for at least a few hours—which was fine with him.

"There's *always* a plan B," he assured Zoe. "But

right now, there's someplace I have to go first. I'd drop you off at home," he told her honestly, "but the last time I did that, it didn't turn out too well."

"I wouldn't have stayed at your house even if you did drop me off," she told him. "After what just happened with Johnny, I intend to stick to you like glue for the next day or two. Or longer," she added for good measure.

He grinned at her. "Might prove to be interesting." And then he grew serious as he warned her, "As long as you make sure not to do something independent and foolhardy." He could just see her charging Vine to make him pay for what he was doing to them.

"The thought never even crossed my mind," she told Sam solemnly.

And if he believed that, Sam thought, grinning, then *he'd* be the naive one.

Chapter 19

"I was beginning to think you stood me up, boy," Matthew Colton's voice crackled with a touch of cynicism as he watched his son cross to him.

They were meeting in the usual place, but this time it was per the specific instructions the senior Colton had set down if the "game" was to go forward.

"Where's Juliet?" he asked, looking past Sam toward the vicinity of the door the latter had used to enter the room. "Has she gotten tired of you already?" Matthew sneered.

Sam refused to say anything more than was absolutely necessary.

"You said you wanted to see me, so here I am." He sat down opposite his father. "I've lived up to my end of it, you live up to yours."

"What, no preemptive chitchat?" Matthew asked mockingly. "No pretense at being the dutiful son at long last?"

Sam felt as if he was operating on the hairy edge. He'd come perilously close to losing Zoe and he was in no mood to play along with whatever game the old man had in mind.

"Cut the bull, old man. You were never interested in anything about us. We all know you're doing this strictly to entertain yourself," Sam said in disgust. "It's your one last pathetic play for power."

The squinting eyes narrowed into tiny, angry slits. "Careful, boy. You hurt my feelings and you go home empty-handed."

"And what do I go home with if I *don't* hurt your feelings?" Sam asked pointedly.

He was beginning to doubt that even if he and his siblings did jump through every hoop Matthew held up, the old man would give them the information they wanted at the end of the game.

"Why, your clue, of course. Clue number one," Matthew emphasized dramatically.

"All right, I'm listening," Sam said, his eyes pinning his father's.

For a long moment, it seemed like the meeting had disintegrated into a staring contest.

Just when Sam was about to declare the whole thing a colossal waste of his time, Matthew said a single word.

"Texas."

Sam blinked, certain he'd heard wrong. "What?"

"Texas," Matthew repeated, this time a little more clearly.

Sam waited, but nothing else followed. Not one extra word.

"That's it?" he questioned incredulously.

Matthew looked at him smugly, very satisfied with the reaction his clue had received.

"That's it."

Sam blew out a breath. He felt frustrated to say the least, but since the old man had made such a point of all this, he assumed that what he was being told was that his mother was buried somewhere in Texas, a state whose land mass was only exceeded by one other state in the union: Alaska.

It wasn't much, but it was a start, Sam thought.

Hopefully, his brothers and sister would be told words that would eventually pull the whole thing into context.

Having given Matthew a sufficient amount of time to say anything additional by way of a clue, Sam rose from the table.

"Okay, then. I'll be seeing you, old man."

"One more thing," Matthew called out after him when he was more than halfway to the door.

Turning around, Sam looked at him. He knew his father was only doing this—adding postscripts when he was almost out of the room—to prove he could yank him around whenever he wanted to.

"Yes?" Sam asked impatiently.

"Since I'm feeling generous, I'll throw you another bone," Matthew told him, drawing his words out so slowly, they felt as if they were crawling along the floor. "Those letters you took from me? The ones I *lent* you?" Matthew reminded him.

He wasn't going to get into a debate unless he knew what the subject was ahead of time.

"Yes?" Sam asked warily.

"Well, if I were you, boy, I'd only be looking at the ones from women." He laughed to himself. "They are the deadlier of the species."

Sam cut across the floor quickly. There was more to what his father was saying, he would have sworn to it. "What else do you know, old man?"

Matthew's expression was defiant. He held all the cards and he knew it.

"I know I'm tired now, so run along, boy. Go," he emphasized, turning the single word into an order.

Sam turned on his heel and walked to the door.

It wasn't much of a clue, he thought as he left the communal room. At least, not the first clue. The second, regarding the serial killer, might actually lead to something, he thought.

It still mystified him that his father was actually willing to just "give away" the information, without trying to trade it for anything more substantial than the things he'd already asked for.

Although, now that he thought of it, beyond what Matthew had already requested—the extended TV privileges, the pillow and some food delicacies—what else would a man in his condition require once freedom was permanently off the table?

* * *

"Well, what did he say?" Zoe asked eagerly, hurrying over to him the minute she saw Sam walk out of the communal room. She'd been sitting in the waiting area, counting the minutes until his return.

Sam slipped his arm around her shoulders. Just feeling her next to him helped ground him. "He asked where you were."

"He didn't," she scoffed, convinced Sam was teasing her.

"Yeah, he did, actually," Sam told her as they made their way out of the area and toward the exit. "He called you 'Juliet.'"

"Did he say anything meaningful?" she pressed.

She knew how much it meant to Sam and the others to be able to eventually reclaim their mother's body and give the poor woman a proper burial the way she deserved.

Sam laughed shortly. "He said the word *Texas*."

"Texas," Zoe repeated, trying to make sense out of the so-called "clue."

"As in that's where he was?"

Sam shrugged. "No, as in that's where he buried my mother, I guess."

"He didn't hint *where* in Texas?" she asked hopefully, even though she knew Matthew Colton wasn't the type to give anything away, even a clue, unless he was well compensated for it.

Sam frowned as he led the way out of the building. "That would have made him human and I learned a long time ago that the old man was, and is, a lot of things. 'Human' was never one of them." There wasn't a drop of compassion in the man. "He did say that when going through his letters, we should be looking at the ones from his female admirers."

"Well, *that's* something," Zoe said, excited.

"I hope," Sam qualified. Where the old man was concerned, he took nothing for granted and reserved even the mere idea of breaking into a happy dance until the final verdict was in. "But right now, I've got something more important to attend to."

She stopped walking for a moment and looked at him quizzically. "Oh?"

Taking her hand in his, Sam resumed leading her to where he'd parked his vehicle. "Plan B," he said mysteriously.

"Which is?" she prodded.

"Hopefully going down soon," he answered, still refraining from elaborating just to tease her.

"What's the penalty for beating on a detective?" she wanted to know.

Sam laughed. She made him feel good. Despite everything that was going on, Zoe made him feel human, something he'd almost forgotten he was capable of feeling.

"That depends on who's doing the beating and how hard," he replied. And then, because she'd been through a lot already and had come through it all without a single complaint or recrimination, he told her, "I'll fill you in on the way in the car."

She nodded, relieved he wasn't going to be close-mouthed about the information. "I have a feeling this is going to be some car ride."

It was all very simple, actually, she realized once Sam explained it to her. The moment he'd found the key Vine was so desperate to get his hands on, he had it taken to the largest hardware store in the two counties and analyzed. The key maker there informed the police officer it was a locker key.

Specifically, it was the kind used for lockers found in an airport.

That, Sam told her as they drove to the county airport, gave his team the focal point for their stakeout.

"Lots of boring downtime spent trying *not* to fall asleep," was the way Sam referred to it.

Zoe, however, saw it as the final moments that just might bring closure to an elusive puzzle.

Sam parked his vehicle as close as he could to the center of the airport while still managing to get some shade so they didn't wind up roasting.

Shutting off the engine, he turned to her. "Okay, here're the rules. The minute I get the call that Vine's been spotted in the airport, I'm going to join the takedown. *You,*" he emphasized, "are going to remain in the car and wait for me. The second I leave, I want you to lock the car, understood?"

She wanted to protest that there had to be something she could do to help, but one look at the expression on Sam's face and she knew she might as well save her breath. She had her marching orders, or, in this case, her sitting orders. If she argued the point with him, Sam might even get someone to either take her home, or, at the very least, sit in the car with her as if she were two years old.

So, she said the only thing she could under the circumstances. "Understood."

"Good." No sooner did he brush his lips against her forehead than his cell phone started to ring. He lost no time extracting it out of his pocket. "Colton."

"Sir, Vine was spotted in the north end of the airport. Looks like he's heading toward the lockers. He's wearing a gray hoodie and torn jeans."

"On my way," Sam responded. Within a second, he was opening the door. "You stay," he said, issuing Zoe her final orders just before he slammed the door and ran for the main terminal.

Had he not spat out the commands as if he were training a pet dog, she might have abided by the agreement they had just struck. But he had and it rankled her. So much so she began imagining all sorts of scenarios being played out inside the terminal, none of them ending well for Sam.

She couldn't just sit here, waiting. She knew he wanted her to, but she couldn't do it. Somewhere along the line since this had all started with Celia's murder, she had ceased being the passive good little soldier she'd always been. Inactivity no longer suited her. So, less than five minutes after Sam had left her and entered the airport, she got out of the car and headed for the central terminal.

Zoe vaguely knew where the lockers were located. She'd been to the airport just once before in her life, to pick up a friend who was flying back for a visit. Knowing how slowly things had a tendency to move, she assumed the airport hadn't been remodeled since then, which meant the lockers were still located where they had been previously: at the east end of the central terminal.

She was just about to go there when someone suddenly grabbed her arm from behind and yanked her around, all but knocking the air out of her.

"Well, well, well, here we are again. Seems like old times, doesn't it?" She found herself looking up into Vine's face. His voice was friendly enough, but his eyes were malevolent. "Nice of you to volunteer to be my insurance policy, especially since it worked out so well for all of us last time."

"Let go of me," Zoe cried. Incredibly, she felt more angry than afraid at the moment.

She yanked hard, trying to get free, but Vine's grip on her arm tightened even more. She felt as if her arm was caught in a vise.

"Yeah, right," Vine snapped, dragging her with him. "Hey, Colton," he yelled out.

The moment he did, people began looking in his direction. The sight of his drawn gun had them instantly screaming and running away in panic. Within seconds, the floor of the central terminal was cleared.

"I know you and your two-bit team are out there. Anyone makes a move toward me, you know the drill. Celia's sister dies. I just want what's coming to me, nothing more. You let me get it and everybody goes home happy—and breathing," he emphasized.

He was hurting her as he dragged her with him, but she wouldn't give Vine the satisfaction of saying so. Instead, she glared at him as she accused, "You killed Celia."

"The hell I did," Vine retorted. The denial surprised her. "Throw away my life just to kill that bitch? She's not worth a week in jail, let alone a life sentence—or the death penalty. No, sweetheart, somebody else killed your slut of a sister, not me," Vine informed her.

Holding her so tightly around her waist now that he all but cut off her air supply, Vine managed to fish the key out of his pocket while still holding his gun trained on her.

"Okay, here's the key. Open the locker and take out what's inside. And remember, you do as I say and no one gets hurt, including that Lone Ranger of yours. Get the least bit creative and it won't just be you I'll be shooting at."

Sam stepped out from around the lockers, his handgun trained on the man holding Zoe prisoner. "Put the gun down, Vine!" he ordered.

"You first," Vine shouted back. "And remember, you might get me, but she's the first casualty. You wanna risk that?" he taunted Sam. "You put your gun down and everyone goes their own way, nice and tidy. I just want what's in the locker," he reiterated. "Now open the damn thing!" he told Zoe. "And ease it out slowly. Once you've got it, we're going to back out of here. Nobody else is going to make a move. Right?" he barked.

"Right," Zoe agreed, the inside of her mouth so dry, it felt as if the word was literally sticking to the roof of her mouth as she uttered it.

Zoe did as he ordered and opened the locker. She was surprised her hands didn't shake. Everything inside of her felt as if it was.

There was a box inside the locker. The same kind she'd seen used as a safety deposit box in a bank. Raising the lid just a crack, she saw that there was something inside the box that looked like cellophane-wrapped bricks of narcotics. She closed the lid.

Taking hold of the box, she slowly drew it out.

She had one chance at this, Zoe thought. Vine might very well mean to let them all go, but she doubted it would go off without a hitch. It was more than likely that someone was going to get hurt and the thought that it might be Sam was more than she could bear.

"Here!" she cried and instead of holding on to the box the way he'd instructed her to do as he backed the two of them out of the terminal, she suddenly swung around and slammed the long metal box into him, clipping him against his chin and his chest at the same time.

Vine howled in pain from the impact. The unexpected blow was enough to completely throw him off balance.

At the same time, the gun discharged, its bullet going wild, and as Vine screamed in pain, Sam and his team rushed the man from all sides.

This time, there was no getting away.

"I told you to stay in the car!" Sam shouted at her as Vine was being cuffed and then hauled away.

Stunned, Zoe stared at him. "That's all you have to say to me?"

"I ought to wring your neck," Sam cried. When he thought of what could have happened to her, how this all might have gone down, he felt sick to the pit of his stomach.

"Nice follow-up," she quipped. "I think Celia was trying to keep these drugs out of circulation… Maybe she did have some redeeming qualities."

"Maybe," Sam agreed.

Suddenly Sam pulled her into his arms, holding her as if he was never going to let her go again. In that one instance, as if the exchange the other day hadn't been enough to bring the point home to him, he realized he wouldn't have been able to survive losing her like that.

Or losing her at all, period.

"Don't you ever, *ever* do that to me again," he warned her, his anger still fresh and hot.

"You're getting better," she told him as if weighing the validity of his response to her help in bringing

Vine down against what he'd just said about wringing her neck.

Then, despite the fact that his men were still in the terminal and there was an abundance of loose ends that still needed tying up, Sam gave in to his own inner needs and kissed her.

Kissed Zoe with every fiber of his being.

Kissed her as if he knew that, had it gone down any other way, he wouldn't have ever been able to kiss her again.

When he drew back for a moment to get his bearings, he saw the wide smile on Zoe's face.

"Much, much better," she pronounced, her eyes shining.

"I can do even better than that," he told her in a low whisper. His heart felt full enough to burst. It was an entirely new feeling for him and he was savoring it as much as he could.

Zoe tilted her head up as she looked at him. "Show me," she whispered.

And he did.

Epilogue

Once Johnny Vine was taken to the police station, booked and secured behind bars, Sam met with his brothers and Annabel. He wanted to pass along the single word that Matthew Colton had volunteered in exchange for his agreed-upon visit.

It would be a full month before the next one of them was to follow in his footsteps, sit down with Matthew and wait until the old man deigned to offer another so-called clue. The arrangement, as the others saw it, was not exactly a satisfactory one, but for now, it was the best they could hope for.

Opinions were mixed as to whether or not they were being played by the man who was, at least biologically, their father.

Some chose to believe, as Zoe had, that faced with his swiftly approaching morality, Matthew had finally decided to make some sort of amends and attempt to live up to his role as their father.

Others were of the opinion that an old dog, especially one that was a rogue, couldn't be taught new tricks.

In this case, only time—if indeed the old man actually had enough left—would tell.

And although finding the location of his mother's remains was very important to him, as was finding his missing sister, Josie, Sam had an equally, slightly more pressing matter he wanted to attend to and hopefully resolve.

It involved Zoe.

The moment he was finished with meeting with his family, Sam hurried back to her house to see her, putting police work on temporary hold.

The second he rang her doorbell, Zoe opened the door. "How did it go with your family?" she wanted to know.

"They're skeptical, like I am," he told her, coming in. "But we don't have much of a choice. We have to play along with his game, just in case he is telling the truth and these pieces do add to up a final location.

"I've also been thinking about this new serial killer the old man seems to have inspired. I think he knows more about the killer than he's saying—and he seems pretty convinced the killer's a woman, not a man. Which means Vine's really not our killer," Sam reluctantly reiterated the conclusion they had already come to. "He's a low-life drug dealer and now a cop killer, but he's not the serial killer we've been looking for."

There was only one conclusion to be drawn from

that. "That means that whoever killed those four victims is still out there, killing women alphabetically for some insane reason." His own words sounded incredibly strange to his ear, but they were also true, which only made the matter that much more horrific.

"Unchecked," he continued, "this loon could really get into full swing." Which brought him to the point of all this. "You're going to need protection, Zoe," Sam told her.

She was touched by his concern, but he was overlooking a very salient point. "I'd like to think that the combined efforts of the Granite Gulch police department and the FBI, not to mention the combined efforts of the rather impressive Colton clan, would catch this deranged serial killer before he gets to the letter *Z*. Besides, maybe you haven't noticed," she went on to point out, "but I don't have dark brown hair. I'm a blonde."

"Oh, I've noticed," he assured her. "I've noticed everything there is to notice about you. And, in all probability, what you said is true. Male or female, we'll wind up catching this killer before all the letters of the alphabet are gone through. But I've never been known for my optimism," he reminded her. "Which means I don't like to take any unnecessary chances. And leaving you unguarded is definitely taking an unnecessary chance. You never know when this nutjob might decide to switch things around and start doing away with twentysomething blondes."

"So you're doing what?" she wanted to know, "Posting a round-the-clock guard on me?"

Sam slipped his arms around her, drawing her closer to him. Inhaling her scent and invigorating his very being by that simple act.

"In a manner of speaking," he allowed.

"What kind of a manner of speaking?" she gently prodded.

Sam took a breath. *Now or never.* "Zoe Robison, will you marry me?"

She looked at him, stunned. This was something she'd dreamed about longer than she could remember. Something she'd fantasized about. But never in her wildest dreams did she ever expect any of it would actually come true.

"Sam, you don't have to do this."

"That all depends on your definition of 'have to,'" he told her. "But I do know that I want to. Now, if *you* don't want to, I understand. Becoming a Colton carries a certain stigma with it for some people, so if you don't feel—"

"Yes."

It took a second for the word to register in his brain. "What?"

"Stop talking," she told him, then repeated, "Yes."

"Yes, you agree it carries a certain stigma, or—"

She decided that saying anything further would just get them bogged down with words. In this case, actions spoke louder than words, so she threw her arms around his neck, rose up on her toes and pressed her lips against his. Hard.

Her message came across, loud and clear.

Sam stopped talking.

* * * * *

COLTON COPYCAT KILLER by Marie Ferrarella

Look for the next thrilling installment in the new COLTONS OF TEXAS *miniseries, coming in February 2016!*

And if you loved this novel, don't miss other suspenseful titles by Marie Ferrarella:

SECOND CHANCE COLTON
HOW TO SEDUCE A CAVANAUGH
CAVANAUGH FORTUNE
CARRYING HIS SECRET

Available now from Harlequin Romantic Suspense!

COMING NEXT MONTH FROM

HARLEQUIN®

ROMANTIC suspense

Available February 2, 2016

#1883 A Secret in Conard County

Conard County: The Next Generation

by Rachel Lee

FBI special agent Erin Sanders doesn't want Deputy Lance Conroe's protection, even if she needs it. But close quarters—and danger—make her realize that she definitely wants *him*...

#1884 Colton's Surprise Heir

The Coltons of Texas

by Addison Fox

With a serial killer on the loose, pregnant Lizzie Connor turns to the one man who can keep her safe—the father of her unborn child, cowboy Ethan Colton.

#1885 Rock-a-Bye Rescue

by Beth Cornelison and Karen Whiddon

When a maniacal cult leader is overthrown, two women team up with men from their pasts to watch over the innocent through the dangerous fallout. Lila Greene must depend on bad boy Dean Hamilton to guard the infant in her care, while Michelle Morgan and FBI agent Garrett Ware protect her nephew from peril.

#1886 Bodyguard Daddy

Bachelor Bodyguards

by Lisa Childs

For a year, Milek Kozminski grieved the loss of his ex-fiancée and their son. But when he learns they're alive, the bodyguard will do anything to keep them that way—and protect them at all costs...

YOU CAN FIND MORE INFORMATION ON UPCOMING HARLEQUIN® TITLES, FREE EXCERPTS AND MORE AT WWW.HARLEQUIN.COM.

HRSCNM0116

When pregnant Lizzie Connor is threatened by a serial killer, she's desperate to keep herself and her unborn child safe. So Lizzie turns to the one man who can protect her—sexy cowboy Ethan Colton, who's also the father of her baby! As sparks fly, danger and true love rear their heads...

Read on for a sneak preview of
COLTON'S SURPRISE HEIR by Addison Fox
the second book in the 2016
***COLTONS OF TEXAS** series.*

"Did you—" Lizzie broke off, her voice heavy and out of breath as she came through the door.

"He's gone."

"He?"

"I thought." Ethan stopped and turned back toward the window. The figure had vanished, but he conjured up the image in his mind. "He was wearing a thick sweatshirt with the hood up, so I guess it could be anyone. He was too far away to get a sense of height."

"The police will ask what color."

"It was nondescript navy blue." Ethan glanced down at his own sweatshirt, tossed on that morning from a stack of similar clothes in the bottom of his drawer. "Just like I'm wearing. Hell, like half the population wears every weekend."

"It's still something."

Lizzie stood framed inside the doorway, long, curly

waves of hair framing her face, and he stilled. Since he'd seen her the morning before, his emotions had been on a roller coaster through the ups and downs of his new reality.

Yet here she was. Standing in the doorway of their child's room, a warrior goddess prepared to do battle to protect her home. He saw no fear. Instead, all he saw was a ripe, righteous anger, spilling from her in hard, deep breaths.

"Maybe you should sit down?"

"I'm too mad to sit."

"Once again, I'm forced to ask the obvious. Humor me."

He reached for the window, but she stopped him. "Leave it. It's not that cold, and maybe there are fingerprints."

Although he had no doubt the perp had left nothing behind, Ethan did as she requested. She'd already taken a seat in the rocking chair in the corner, and he felt his knees buckle at the image that rose up to replace her in his mind's eye.

Lizzie, rocking in that same chair, their child nestled in her arms, suckling at her breast.

The shock of emotion that burrowed beneath his heart raced through him, and Ethan fought to keep any trace of it from showing. How could he feel so much joy at something so unexpected?

At something he'd never wanted?

HRSEXP0116

Love the Harlequin book you just read?

Your opinion matters.

Review this book on your favorite book site, review site, blog or your own social media properties and share your opinion with other readers!

JUST CAN'T GET ENOUGH?

Join our social communities
and talk to us online.

You will have access to the latest news on upcoming titles and special promotions, but most importantly, you can talk to other fans about your favorite Harlequin reads.

Harlequin.com/Community

Facebook.com/HarlequinBooks

Twitter.com/HarlequinBooks

Pinterest.com/HarlequinBooks